RUNNING ON EMPTY

RUNNING
ON EMPTY

S.E. Durrant

Holiday House   New York

First published in the UK in 2018 by Nosy Crow Ltd, London
First published in the USA in 2018 by Holiday House, New York
Printed and Bound in July 2018 at Maple Press, York, PA, USA
www.holidayhouse.com
First American Edition
1 3 5 7 9 10 8 6 4 2

Library of Congress Cataloging-in-Publication Data

Names: Durrant, S. E., author.
Title: Running on empty / by S. E. Durrant.
Description: First American edition. ǀ New York : Holiday House, 2018.
Originally published: London : Nosy Crow Ltd, 2018. ǀ Summary: After
his grandfather dies, eleven-year-old AJ, a talented runner, assumes
new responsibilities including taking care of his intellectually-
challenged parents and figuring out how bills get paid.
Identifiers: LCCN 2017035204 ǀ ISBN 9780823438402 (hardcover)
Subjects: ǀ CYAC: Family life—England—Fiction. ǀ People with mental
disabilities—Fiction. ǀ People with disabilities—Fiction. ǀ Running—
Fiction. ǀ Death—Fiction. ǀ Responsibility—Fiction.
England—Fiction.
Classification: LCC PZ7.1.D875 Run 2018 ǀ DDC [Fic]—dc23 LC record
available at https://lccn.loc.gov/2017035204

"It's no use going back to yesterday, because
I was a different person then."
Alice's Adventures in Wonderland
by Lewis Carroll

CENTER OF THE UNIVERSE

The most amazing thing I ever saw was Usain Bolt winning the 100 meters at the London Olympics. I was there with my mum, dad, and grandad and we were high up in the stadium and I was seven years old and I felt like I was at the center of the universe. And when he broke the Olympic record I thought the noise would lift the stadium up off the ground and catapult it right out into space. Because nothing about that moment felt ordinary.

And one of the most unforgettable things about it—and not the best—was when people ran to the front and pushed forward for autographs, and there was Amit from my class. He just popped up on the big screen. He was enormous. His head was the height of the high jump. He was trying to squeeze through to the barrier and he was just desperate to touch Usain Bolt or get his autograph on his ticket. And he did. He pushed right to the front.

I felt sort of annoyed. I hadn't even known he was there. I tried not to let it bother me but it did. And it's sort of bugged me ever since. I just had to not look too hard when Amit got right up close to Usain Bolt, and when he got his autograph I thought I'd be sick. I'm not kidding. I nearly threw up. I was thinking maybe I should run down to the front too and try to catch Usain when he did his lap of honor. He had the Jamaican flag around his shoulders and he didn't look in any hurry to get out of the stadium. But then I thought no, I might be too late. And it would be so embarrassing if I got caught on TV as the boy who tried to run down and couldn't get through. So I just sat there and Amit looked right into the camera and he was beaming from ear to ear like he'd just won the golden ticket in *Charlie and the Chocolate Factory.*

I would have done anything for that autograph and I still would, to tell you the truth, even though I'm eleven years old now. I tried to concentrate on what I already had, which I guess was something more spiritual. I felt like I had a connection with Usain Bolt and having Amit there sort of spoiled it. I think Usain Bolt probably felt more spiritual too. He was probably annoyed with all these people trying to get close to him, though he seemed to be quite enjoying it. He's good with the crowd.

Anyway, Amit got the autograph and I didn't and he took it to school at the start of Year 3 and did a talk about how Usain Bolt gave him a special look when he signed his ticket. It was sickening. But that's Amit for you. He's better-looking and cleverer than everyone else and he always gets what he wants. I expect every school's got a kid like that.

And on the whole I've managed to turn that moment around in my head and make myself feel badly about Amit getting the autograph. I think, *Why couldn't he just stay in his seat and enjoy the moment? What was the matter with him?* It's funny how you can change the way you feel if you put your mind to it.

And the thing about that race is it really was special for me because the Olympic Stadium is just a few streets from our house. We saw them build it. Honestly. We're that close. And another reason it was special is Usain Bolt won in 9.63 seconds and Grandad lived at number 9 and we live down the road at number 63. I sometimes think if Grandad had lived at number 8 Usain Bolt might have run the 100 meters in 8.63 seconds and if Grandad had lived at number 7 and Usain Bolt had won the race in 7.63 seconds, the world would have physically exploded because it would have been a miracle. I know that might sound stupid but it's just a feeling I've got.

But usually when I think of Usain Bolt winning

the 100 meters I think of Mum shouting at the top of her voice and Dad with his eyes shut and his hands over his ears and Grandad squeezing my hand and saying, *Can you believe it, AJ?* and me just knowing I would remember that moment for the rest of my life.

BUZZING

I'm going to tell you what makes me different straightaway. If I don't, it sort of buzzes around at the back of my brain like a fly stuck in a room. And that bugs me. You know that thing where they bang against the window and you just have to let them out because they're keeping you from thinking about anything else? Well, that's how it feels. So what I do is, either I open the window and let the fly buzz out into the world, or I decide to never, ever let the fly out and eventually it stops buzzing. It depends who I'm talking to.

The thing that makes me different from other eleven-year-old boys, apart from my fantastic running ability, is my parents have learning difficulties. It's no big deal for me. Really it isn't. I don't look after them. We look after each other.

My mum makes the best cakes ever. She's the kindest person in the world too. Honestly, you'd know if you met her. She might not have an easy time making sense of lots of things all at once, but she's clever in the way of understanding bigger things better than most people. She doesn't waste years of her life sending messages or texting. She doesn't do any of that. She won't even answer the phone. She talks to people if they're with her but apart from that she can't be bothered. And she doesn't spend tons of time worrying either. She worries about something and then she stops worrying and then she's happy.

When I worry I'm awake all night and in the morning my head hurts and my stomach aches and I can't concentrate at school. And I'm supposed to be clever. Not brilliant but sort of okay. But when Mum gets up she's smiling. Even though there's lots to worry about, she's smiling. So who's smarter?

My dad's more like me in the way of worrying. He just can't stop. If he's worried, he walks up and down the garden, even if it's the middle of the night. He just walks up and down, up and down, between the vegetables.

My dad practically lives in the garden. If you came to our house you might not see him unless you looked out the kitchen window, and then you might just see the top of his hat poking out from behind the beans. He grows potatoes, onions, beans, pumpkins, spinach, and garlic. And if that makes you think we've got a big garden, we haven't. It's seven steps from our kitchen door to our back fence. I'm not kidding. One more step and you'd knock yourself out. Dad just grows everything really close together. Grandad taught him that.

My mum has four rules for life. My dad has one. My mum's are:

Be kind to people.

Do your best.

Make sure everything's switched off.

Remember to look at the sky.

My dad's rule is:

Love Alice (that's my mum).

As for any other rules, he follows hers. She's the most important person in the world to him. They are like two halves of a whole. They fit perfectly. They're just not so good at dealing with stuff like sorting out forms or if the washing machine needs fixing. My grandad did all that. That's my mum's dad.

My grandad lived down the road but he died two months ago. Just before school ended for the summer. And I know it really wasn't my fault, but sometimes I think maybe he died because of me. And that makes me feel so bad. Because I was the last one to see him alive.

100 METERS IS 100 METERS

My grandad was always running. Even when he was old he never really stopped. When I was eight I said, *Can I come too?* and he said yes. He was pretty pleased, I think. And those times running with him were some of the happiest times of my life. I'm not kidding.

We've got this little park around the corner and

we went to it one day and measured the path like a running track. Grandad had a little pot of red paint and a tiny paintbrush and he just knelt down and made a dot every 100 meters in exactly the right place. He didn't even pretend not to do it. He just painted a dot and nobody seemed to notice.

We worked out that it's 100 meters from the flower bed to the dog-poo bin, 100 meters from the dog-poo bin to halfway down the bench, 100 meters from halfway down the bench to the broken tree, and 100 meters from the broken tree to the shelter with the graffiti. We went around the path twice and marked out 1,000 meters, all in exactly the right places. I'd tell you more about it but it's probably best if you come yourself, if you want to see. Because it sounds quite boring but it really isn't boring at all.

And the best thing about our track is Grandad said it's exactly the same as the Olympic track because 100 meters is 100 meters wherever it is.

Anyway, last time I saw Grandad he just ran from the dog-poo bin to the bench and then he said, "I'm going to have to go home, AJ. I'm not feeling too good."

I said, "Please, Grandad, just a bit more. You can sit on the bench."

But he shook his head.

"No, AJ. Got to go."

And then he smiled. "See if you can beat your record," he said.

And as he walked away he didn't even look back. He just walked down the shortcut through the bushes and he was gone. I was quite disappointed to be honest but I jogged around the park a few times and then I ran 400 meters in about 60 seconds. It was my fastest time ever. I couldn't wait to tell him, I knew he'd be really impressed.

But when I got to his house he wouldn't answer the door. My aunt Josephine and my cousin Aisha were at my place, so Mum and Josephine went to Grandad's with the spare keys and I stayed at home and looked after Aisha (the best kid in the world by the way). And they found Grandad dead. He'd just sat down on his chair and he was dead. And although the doctor said he had a weak heart and he was lucky to live so long it doesn't feel lucky at all.

One funny thing though. Mum and Josephine said he was smiling when they found him. They even said it at the funeral. I don't know what they meant exactly. I didn't see him myself. But I think about it sometimes. I think about all sorts of things in fact. Sometimes I think, *What if he'd sat on the bench and waited for me?* He might have died there and that would have been worse. I'd have come running around the bend and he could have been dead on the bench. And he would not have liked that. It might have been on the news. It would have been terrible in lots of ways. Social services might have come around.

Josephine said the way Grandad died was the best way. She said if only everyone could go like that, like dying in your chair is a dream come true. It's the sort of depressing thing grown-ups say. It made me feel awful because Grandad wasn't depressed at all. I don't think he wanted to die in his chair. Not then anyway. He was only seventy-two. Maybe if he was a hundred he wouldn't have minded.

Anyway, in case you don't know what it's like to lose someone you love I'll tell you. You can't even understand how your heart keeps beating or why people are acting like it's an ordinary day when actually it feels like the end of the world. And you can't imagine how you're going to be able to keep putting one foot in front of the other for the rest of your whole long life. You can't even imagine it.

Mum was so sad she didn't speak for days. Dad doesn't talk much anyway, so that didn't change, but his face looked like all the bones had fallen out and his head was collapsing onto his shoulders. And when I saw them like that I realized Grandad had been right at the center of our family, and now there was a huge space where he used to be. And that's when I decided I was going to fill that space and sort everything out just like he did.

And I'm going to keep putting one foot in front of the other too, even though it's hard, and I'm going to do it fast. Because I'm a runner like my grandad and one day I'm going to run on a track in a stadium. Maybe even the Olympic Stadium. That would be amazing.

THE BEST RUNNING SHOES
IN THE WORLD

I'm running so fast my feet don't touch the ground.
I don't notice at first. I think I must be wearing the
best running shoes in the world and then I realize
I'm sort of flying. And someone shouts "Look at
that boy!" and the crowd roars and I can't even see
where I'm running because I'm going so fast everything's a blur. All I know is at this moment I'm the
happiest, fastest, most brilliant eleven-year-old boy
in the world. And somewhere Grandad's watching.

And then I'm back in the real world because I
wasn't really running so fast I was flying, I was sitting on my bed gazing into space. And now Mum's
put the kettle on and the switch is broken so if you

don't turn the kettle off by pulling out the plug the steam comes all the way up the stairs. That's how small our house is. And I can't stand it. I'm not kidding. I can't stand the kettle bubbling away on its own like it's going to explode.

I run down to the kitchen and pull the cord out. The back door's open. Mum's standing in the garden with Dad looking at the sunflowers. She sees me and smiles.

"AJ," she says. "Thank you."

She looks at Dad.

"That's kind, isn't it, Eddie?"

Dad nods.

"Yup," he says.

"Very kind," says Mum.

We got the tallest sunflowers ever this year. They're drooping now and a squirrel keeps stealing the seeds but they still look amazing.

It's sort of disappointing to wake up from a daydream. Because I'm not on a track with a crowd of people cheering me on, I'm in a little house with creaky stairs and a leaking roof and I'm pouring boiling water into Mum's chipped teapot. I couldn't even spin around in my room if I wanted to. I'd knock myself out. Maybe that's why I've got such a big imagination.

When Mum and Dad come in we sit around the table. Mum looks worried. She's got this thing where a cloud passes right above her face and she's suddenly in shadow. And it's going across her face now.

My cousin Aisha's got the same thing. You can see all her emotions all the time.

Mum holds out a letter.

"Can you read this, AJ?" she says.

For a horrible moment I think I'm in trouble at school, even though I've only been there three weeks. But when I open the envelope there's a letter with a picture of a tap at the top with drops of water falling out like balloons. At the bottom of the page it says *Total due: £122.46.*

Grandad used to sort out our bills because Mum and Dad aren't good at reading, so now it's my job. I don't mind though. I'm going to be the only kid in Year 7 who knows how much it costs to boil a kettle or leave a light on. (When I've worked it out, that is.)

"Do we have to pay for water?" I say.

"I suppose so," Mum says. "Someone has to put it in the taps."

"For the garden," says Dad.

"And for all the baths we have," Mum says. "Except you don't have any, AJ."

(She's exaggerating.)

"But is it okay?" she says.

For a moment I feel a little shiver of worry because I'm not sure if it's okay but then I remember something Grandad told me about bills. He said red bills mean trouble. I don't know what kind of trouble exactly. Someone probably takes your water away or even your house. Anyway, this bill's not red. It's black writing on white paper.

I hold it up so Mum and Dad can see.

"It's fine," I say. "It's only a problem if it's red and there's not a single bit of red on this one."

Mum laughs. The cloud disappears and the sun comes out.

"That's all right, isn't it, Eddie?" she says. "It's not a red one."

Dad nods. He's looking at the garden. The squirrel's back. It's climbed the tallest sunflower and it's pulling out seeds and stuffing them into its cheeks. We don't stop it. We never do. We don't want it to be hungry.

GRANDAD'S ASHES

It's the end of summer and the wind blows litter down the curb. Dad's buttoned his coat up to his chin and pulled his hat down over his ears. Mum's made a chocolate cake.

We're going to the river to scatter Grandad's ashes. We've been putting it off because no one really wanted to do it, so they've been sitting next to the radiator in a big ugly gray plastic jar.

But then Mum said, "Can we put these somewhere else? They don't feel like Grandad."

I said, "Don't worry, they might not even be Grandad; they could be anyone." But that made her feel even worse.

Dad's carrying the ashes. Mum puts her arm

through his and I trail behind like a weird long shadow. (I'm taller than them already.) Dad's nervous because he only used to go out if Grandad went with him and it doesn't really count with him being in a jar.

Our street's full of little row houses with trash bins and bikes squeezed in front and right at the end is Grandad's house. There's scaffolding across the front now and a Dumpster full of his old kitchen cupboards, where he used to keep his biscuits and his tea bags and where Mum and Josephine used to hide when they were little. We all shudder as we walk past.

We turn the corner and walk down to the row of shops. When we get to the convenience store I stare at the pavement as if there's the most fascinating bit of chewing gum stuck between the cracks. Because there's this girl who works in there and she's so beautiful I can't even look at her. And I know she probably doesn't notice me, but in case she does I don't want her to see me trailing behind my parents like a giraffe. Because I might even marry her one day. Not yet, obviously, but it's just a feeling I've got.

The Olympic Park is amazing. It's got gigantic mobiles and lines of flags and everything's clean and new. The stadium's there and the Olympic pool and the velodrome and the BMX track and a huge red twisting metal tower with a slide so you can go from the top to the bottom at about a million miles an hour. I haven't been on the slide yet but we're going to get tickets one day. And there are new apartment buildings in bright colors and in the distance there are cranes building more and more. I don't know what they're like inside but on the outside they look like an ad for the future.

My heart starts racing when I see the stadium. I'm not exaggerating. I have to take a deep breath to calm myself down. It looks like a spaceship and it's the real, actual place where Usain Bolt broke the Olympic record. It's sort of unbelievable. I stand for a few moments just looking at it and then I follow Mum and Dad along the river, past some geese trying to get out of the way of a barge.

Aisha, Josephine, and Tyler are sitting on a bench waiting for us. Tyler, by the way, is married to Josephine, which means he's my uncle. He's probably the most boring person in the world to tell you the truth. It's hard to believe he's Aisha's dad because he's no fun at all. It's quite strange really because he's a security guard at the Olympic Stadium, which you'd think would be really exciting. Anyway, he's never excited about anything as far as I can tell.

When they see us Aisha jumps up and runs over. She's wearing a hoodie with ducks on it.

"Why are you wearing that?" I say.

"Because Grandad liked it."

"Did he? Why?"

(Sometimes I can't help being horrible. She's only eight.)

"It was his favorite," she says. "And anyway there's ducks on the river."

Normally she'd stick her tongue out but she doesn't.

Tyler takes the jar from Dad and unscrews the lid. The stuff inside looks like cat litter.

"Is that really Grandad?" Aisha says.

"No," I say, "it's probably the milkman or the bus driver."

"Can you have a little respect, AJ?" says Tyler.

Josephine's really pregnant. She's enormous. She looks like she might have the baby there and then. I'm so much hoping she doesn't. She puts her arm around Mum and they stand together. They look so sad.

Grandad said there used to be loads of factories around here and chimneys pumping out smoke. He said it smelled terrible. I imagine him walking along the river in one of those horrible jackets with the huge lapels people wore in the '60s and trying not to breathe in the smell. He thought it was amazing when the river got cleaned up.

We stand in a circle and take a handful of ashes each.

Josephine says, "Does anyone want to say a few words?"

Mum says, "I do."

Then she says, "I miss you, Dad."

And tears roll down her cheeks and because it's windy they sort of zigzag down her face.

We walk to the edge of the river and throw the ashes into the reeds and just at that moment a gust of wind blows them back at us. Aisha screams and runs along the footpath, Mum's picking bits out of her hair, and we're all sort of laughing but not in a normal way because it feels so weird. Because the ashes really are nothing like Grandad. Honestly they could be anyone at all.

WORMS

Dad goes straight into the garden as soon as we're home. Me and Aisha follow.

"Can I see the worms?" Aisha says.

Dad nods. He's got this huge bin full of worms called a wormery. He puts waste food in, the worms eat it, and it comes out as compost. They're not the most exciting pets in the world, more working pets I suppose. Like sheepdogs, only not as much fun.

He takes off the lid and thousands of worms wriggle like mad. Aisha's sort of peering in and jumping back at the same time.

"Hello, wormies," she says.

"You know they can't hear you?" I say.

"You talk to them, don't you, Eddie?" Aisha says.

Dad nods.

"I do," he says.

"But they don't talk back," I say. "You can't even see their faces."

"That makes them perfect," says Aisha.

(Actually I don't even know if they have faces.)

We leave Dad in the garden and squeeze around the kitchen table with Mum, Josephine, and Tyler. Mum's scrubbed the teapot so it's gleaming. It's got little blue flowers on it and even though the lid's chipped it makes her happy. Except today she doesn't look happy. No one does. We're all looking at each other blankly while she cuts the cake. I can't stand it. A funny thing about me is I don't like silence. I've just got to fill it. It's all right if I'm on my own but when I'm with other people I just can't stand it.

"So," I say, "Tyler, how's the stadium?"

"Same as ever, AJ."

"Do you ever want to just run around it?" I say.

He shakes his head.

"I bet you do. I can just imagine all the security guards racing around in their yellow jackets."

Tyler picks up a plate of cake and takes it out to Dad. He's got no sense of humor. He's always grumpy and tired. He loves watching the West Indies play cricket because he can sit down for hours, and he loves fishing because he can have a good sleep there, too. He just sits down next to the river, switches off his phone, and doesn't have to talk to anyone. I don't even know why Josephine married him to be honest. They got married two years ago, even though they've been together forever, because they wanted a special occasion. I thought it was a shame because Josephine could have maybe found someone better.

But what I hate most about Tyler is he won't let me go on the Olympic track, even though he works there. Even though it was the one thing in the whole world I most wanted to do with Grandad, and now it can't ever happen. I have to stop myself from thinking about it. I don't want to make a fuss and spoil the day.

"Mum," I say, "if you had to kill one person to save the world, would you do it?"

"What?" she says.

"Just kill one person to save the whole world. Everyone would die—even me—if you didn't kill that one person."

"What person?"

"It doesn't matter. You're missing the point."

"It matters if I've got to kill them," she shrieks.

"Okay," I say. "Aisha, if you could save the whole world if you threw me to the crocodiles, would you do it?"

Aisha shrugs. She's eating cake.

"Give it a rest, will you?" Josephine says.

Tyler comes back to the table.

"I'll tell you what I'd do," he says. "I'd save the world and let the crocs get you."

He's not smiling. I'd be okay if he was smiling but he's not.

"I might even let the crocs get you if I can't save the world."

Everyone's looking at each other. It's awkward.

"AJ," says Aisha, "can we go to the park?"

I nod. It's an escape. I have to squeeze past Tyler to get out. I don't want to look at him but I do, sort of sideways. He's ugly. I never really understood before, but now I can see he never got out of the ugly-teen stage.

"Come on," says Aisha.

As we walk out my neck is on fire.

BONES AND TEETH AND STUFF

If there's only one person in the park, you can be 99 percent sure it's going to be Victor. You could probably bet your whole life on it. Victor was best man at Grandad's wedding. They even went to school together. It's hard to imagine because I've only ever known him as an old man sitting on the bench feeding the ducks. They should make a statue of him when he dies. Like people leave benches when they die, his could be a bench with him sitting on it with a bag of bread. He waves to us from across the pond and we wave back.

Aisha runs to the swings.

"Do you think if I went really high I'd go over the top?" she says.

I don't know the answer but I'd never tell Aisha that.

"Yeah," I say. "Do you want to try?"

I push her as high as I can and one moment she's screaming and the next she's feeling sick. She jumps off and races back to the gate. When I catch up with her she's got the little cloud over her head.

"AJ," she says, "you know what we did with Grandad?"

"You mean the ashes?"

She nods.

"Was it really him?"

"Maybe."

"But it wasn't anything like him," she says. "What was it?"

"It's all the stuff left over," I say, "from when he was cremated."

"Like bones and teeth and stuff?"

I nod.

"All that's left after you take the water out?"

"Yes, I suppose."

"But if you put the water back it wouldn't be Grandad again."

"No!" I say. (I might be shouting.) "He's not a dried fruit."

Aisha doesn't smile. She's kicking the side of the curb.

"I don't understand," she says.

Tears bubble over her eyes. I crouch down in front of her.

"It wouldn't be Grandad," I say, "because mixed in with all the dry stuff and the water was a little bit of magic."

"And that magic was Grandad?"

I nod.

She stands for a few moments just blinking. Then she says, "Okay." And suddenly she's cartwheeling down the pavement as fast as she can to get out from under that cloud.

ROCKY BOAT

When we get home Mum's putting a lump of cake into a plastic box and Josephine's standing up but looks like she needs to sit down. She's usually quite funny, but since Grandad died she looks like she's in a rocky boat with lots of insects buzzing around her head and she's trying not to throw up.

"AJ," she says, "I've told Alice if you have any problems you're to tell me."

"And I've told Josephine we're fine," says Mum. "She can help us after the baby comes." She beams. "And we can look after the baby."

Mum loves babies.

"I'm just making sure you know too, AJ," says Josephine. "Your mum's far too stubborn. Bit like you."

This sort of thing always happens.

"Just saying," she says.

I'd like to tell Josephine about the water bill actually because it's slightly bothering me. I know it wasn't red but I don't know how many bills you get before they do turn red. And what if the next one is? I don't say anything though. I try to give her a reassuring smile like grown-ups do when you don't know them well enough to tell if they're worried. I don't mean to but I probably look like I'm smirking.

BEATING USAIN BOLT

I tried to run in the park after Grandad died but I felt so bad seeing the red dots and knowing he wasn't there. So what I do now is I run up and down the stairs in my socks. Mostly I do it when Mum's at work because she doesn't like it and after I've been up and down a few times she puts the kettle on and goes into the garden. She knows I'll have to stop to turn off the kettle. It's pretty annoying actually.

We'll be running on the track soon at school and I want to be the fastest. I haven't seen anyone who looks like they might be really fast, except Amit of course. At primary school he always streaked ahead and I'd catch up and then it would be me and him neck and neck to the finish. Sometimes he won and sometimes I did, but I always felt like I had more energy than him. It might not have looked like that from the outside because I get pretty sweaty but that's how I felt.

And in a few weeks there's the Year 7 school cross-country trials and I really want to enter because if I win I'll be chosen to represent the school. And when everyone knows how good I am I'll be one of those kids who trains on the school track and primary-school kids imagine being them. That's going to be me. And everything's going to feel so much better because there won't be an empty space where Grandad used to be.

When I run I get the feeling I could go on and on and never have to stop. I've never got to that point where my legs won't go anymore and my heart's about to explode. If my legs get tired my heart feels fine and then if my heart feels like it's about to explode my legs suddenly feel better. When I run I actually have the feeling I'm the best runner in the world.

I told my friend Crystal once and she said, "What, better than Usain Bolt?" And of course not, because Usain Bolt is crazy-good. He's so good he's almost superhuman. No one can compete with Usain Bolt. But I have a feeling that I could outrun him, just not in the 100 meters. When I tried to explain that to Crystal she looked genuinely sorry for me (which was quite annoying to tell you the truth).

So since then I haven't told anyone else. But it's just a feeling I have. He'd win to begin with of course. He'd shoot off and I'd be left lagging behind. But then he'd get tired. Because he's not built for long distance. And soon he'd be slowing down and his huge muscles would begin to feel too heavy to lift and with every step I'd gradually make up time with him. And then I'd get past him and there he'd be, dragging himself behind me, limbs flailing, getting smaller and smaller in the distance.

That's what I really think. But I keep it to myself now. Sometimes it's enough just to know something's true. You don't always have to prove it. Sometimes you can't. You don't have to go on and on about the way you see the world, trying to make everyone else's mind exactly like yours. Because it doesn't work. People just stop listening.

They've got these posters in school. They're sort of inspirational quotes. They've even got them in the toilets so you can't avoid them. They're staring right at you when you wash your hands or look at yourself in the mirror. There's one that says DREAM BIG, WORK HARD, BE HUMBLE. It's not a rule many people keep at school. But that's what I try to do. It's not easy but I try.

SECONDARY SCHOOL

It's hard to remember what's happened since Grandad died, which is strange because one thing that happened is I started secondary school. And I'd been looking forward to it for years because it's next to my primary school and I was always imagining myself running around the track. But if your grandad just died and you thought he'd live forever, then suddenly nothing seems very important.

So if you want to know about secondary school I can only tell you two things. First, if you're not good at making new friends (I'm not), it helps to have one in your class.

I'm in the same class as Crystal. She's my best friend, which is quite funny as she's much cleverer than me. Sometimes while Crystal's thinking about what's happening to the ozone layer or any of that stuff I'm still trying to work out what the question means. Other people might give up if they had to work as hard as me but I just keep on trying. And when I get the answer I feel like a little bit of light's gone right into my brain.

Me and Crystal met in preschool. We used to hang upside down on the climbing bars while the other kids ran around. And at the end of the day when the parents came to pick us up, my mum would usually wait outside on her own, unless Grandad came. But sometimes Crystal's mum would stand with her. They made quite a pair of opposites because Crystal's mum's tall with a big Afro and my mum's small with the straightest hair in the world and Crystal's mum would be talking and smiling kindly and I don't think my mum said a word. They didn't exactly become friends but me and Crystal did. And we've been best friends ever since.

The second thing I can tell you is don't get a huge

backpack. They're embarrassing. Crystal's is bright orange. Her mum wrote her name on it in felt-tip pen—not the small sort of felt-tip but one with a huge black nib so no one could miss it. Just in case anyone wants to steal it maybe or perhaps in case Crystal wants to pretend it's not hers. I've got my dad's backpack that's about a hundred years old and really small, but I didn't mind that first day because I was just stumbling around waiting to go home. And I still don't mind because all the Year 7s are realizing huge backpacks are really uncool.

And the only thing I remember about my first day is that by the end I felt like I'd been lost in a tunnel and had to crawl my way out. Crystal looked like she'd just been on a picnic. She was almost skipping. I'm not kidding.

"What did you think?" I said.

"I don't mind it so far," she said. "It'll be okay."

"But you're not exactly going to look forward to it, are you?"

"I might."

It made me realize how people see the world completely differently from each other. Even Crystal and she's my friend.

OLYMPIC RUNNER

Miss Charmant's giving everyone a form about parents evening and a letter with our details on it for parents and guardians to check. I'm not even going to think about parents evening (Grandad used to come, Mum and Dad would hate it) so I open the letter and pick up my pen.

"Take it home, AJ," Miss Charmant says. "It's for parents or guardians."

It's lucky she stopped me or I'd be signing it right in front of her. That's how stupid I am.

Charmant, by the way, is French for *charming*, which could be embarrassing except Miss Charmant *is* quite charming. She's my form tutor and I'm in her French class too. I want to learn French because I'm going to live in Canada one day and they speak French there as well as English.

Then Miss Charmant goes around the class asking for everyone's favorite color and favorite food. There's a boy called Harvey who sits next to Crystal and always looks at her with puppy-dog eyes. He's got long, floppy hair and he tries to push it back off his face when he's next to her (it doesn't work).When Crystal says her favorite color's blue he says, "Blue too actually," and when she says her favorite food is fish and chips he says his is fish. I'm thinking it's not a coincidence.

We've just started answering *What do you want to be when you grow up?* when the bell goes. I'm quite relieved actually. I don't want to say Olympic runner because Miss Charmant must have heard that sort of thing a million times. And anyway I want to keep the surprise element. I like to think that one day, when she's not my teacher anymore, she'll be watching the Olympics and she'll see me win gold and she'll think, *That's AJ!!* and her eyes will fall out of her head.

"What do you want to be when you grow up, Harvey?" Crystal says as we walk out.

"A butterfly collector," he says.

He's smiling so much I can't tell if he's joking. He's even more clumsy than me. He's always crashing into things.

"Do you want to collect them alive or dead?" says Crystal.

"Well," he says, "I suppose they're more beautiful alive, fluttering around and all that, but you can see them better when they're dead."

Crystal doesn't look too impressed.

"So both," he says, "but alive first."

TOO BIG FOR MY BRAIN

I think my body's growing too fast. My brain can't keep up. I'm okay at walking as long as I pay attention and I'm brilliant at running because that's my natural talent, but I'm rubbish at all other sports.

We're doing gymnastics in PE—jumping over the pommel horse, climbing the bars, that sort of thing—and I keep stubbing my toes. We do it in bare feet so it hurts. Today I crack my elbow and this horrible numbness shoots down to my fingers.

Mr. Higgins rolls his eyes. He's my PE teacher. He can't help himself. He's that sort of person.

I don't mind though. He's going to be amazed when he sees me run.

MINNIE MOUSE EARS

I'm picking Aisha up from school. Josephine and Tyler both work, so some days Aisha goes to the after-school club where they play games and get snacks, and some days she comes home with me. She's waiting at the gates with a girl wearing Minnie Mouse ears. She looks proud.

"This is a new girl," she says.

The new girl's looking at me suspiciously. Aisha's waiting for me to smile at her friend. So I do.

"This is my cousin. He goes to big school."

Her friend looks impressed.

"Are you a teenager?" she says.

"Nearly."

"What do you mean?"

"I'm eleven."

She doesn't look impressed anymore.

"He's nearly twelve," says Aisha.

The girl puts her hands on her hips.

"He has to be thirteen to be a teenager. All teenagers have 'teen' in their age. That's where it comes from."

Aisha sighs.

"Have you made any new friends yet, AJ?" she says.

I shake my head.

"Is this your new friend?" I say.

I can see she's already getting tired of her.

Aisha shrugs.

"Maybe," she says.

WHY IS THE SKY BLUE?

Me and Aisha always do the same thing when we get in. Aisha runs out to see Dad and the worms. I wave at Dad. Then I make toast. The toaster sets the smoke alarm off so Aisha comes back in and waves a tea towel around until it stops ringing. Then we eat the toast, I do homework, and Aisha pretends to do homework.

I've got French and Science today and I've got the letter with my details to check. It's got all the information Grandad put down when we applied for my school placement, like my birthday and that I'm entitled to free school lunches. Our address is on it but it's got Grandad as the person to contact in an emergency. At the bottom it says *Please sign if this information is correct. If there have been any changes since your child's school application please enter the information below.*

I think about what to do for one nanosecond and then I sign the form. I don't want the school to know

Grandad died in case they think Mum and Dad can't manage and I get taken away. And that's such a terrible thought I do a quick messy scribble for a signature and put the letter in my bag as fast as I can. I don't want to even think about it.

Aisha's drawing. You'd think she was planning brain surgery the way she concentrates. She's got this self-important look on her face but actually she's drawing a house on a hill with little sheep dotted around.

"Why is the sky blue when it's above mountains?" she says.

"What?"

"Why's the sky blue when it hasn't got the sea underneath?"

"What do you mean?"

"When it hasn't got the sea to make it blue."

I don't know what she's talking about. I have to stop and think a moment. Then I get it.

"The sky doesn't reflect the sea," I say. "The sea reflects the sky."

"Does it?"

If she were anyone else, I'd think, *What an idiot.* It makes me realize how young she is.

"Yeah. You don't get blue water, do you? If you put a bit of sea in a glass, it's not blue, is it?"

"No."

"Because the sea's not blue. It's the sky."

She goes to the sink and comes back with a glass of water.

"You're right. It's not blue."

She gulps it down.

"Don't get hiccups," I say.

She gets hiccups all the time.

She colors in a perfect blue sky.

"So why's the sky blue?"

I sort of know but not quite.

"It's complicated," I say.

"Too complicated for you?" she says.

"Yeah, yeah," I say, as though it's not really. "Too complicated for me. I'll find out and get back to you."

She finishes the drawing.

"It's for you, AJ," she says.

It's nice. I love the way little kids draw a line of blue sky at the top of their picture. You can't really do it when you're older. People think you're stupid. But there's something really nice about a line of blue sky.

IMPATIENT

When Josephine arrives to pick up Aisha she's so impatient she's actually stepping from foot to foot. I'm not kidding. She can't wait to get back out the door.

"Can't we wait for Alice to get back?" says Aisha.

"Sorry," Josephine says. "I've got work to do this evening."

Josephine's a bookkeeper, which sounds like she

keeps books but actually means she looks after all the money in a heating company. She has to work out the prices for radiators and pipes and all the stuff that heats your house up. She's having her baby soon so she has to finish everything before she stops work and goes on maternity leave.

"Please," says Aisha. "I'll give you my drawing."

(That's the drawing she's promised me by the way.)

Josephine shakes her head.

"Won't be long," she says, and she pats her belly.

Aisha gives her the drawing anyway. That's what she's like. If you don't grab the picture quickly enough, she gives it to someone else.

SCUTTLING

I must look ridiculous training on the stairs. I try not to think about it too much. I don't want to put myself off. I probably look like a spider scuttling up and down a drainpipe. If an alien from another planet was watching, they wouldn't understand at all, or they might think I'm the engine keeping the fridge whirring.

Anyway, I run up and down fifty-eight times until my head's throbbing and my feet are slipping. A couple of times I land on my knees. That's fifty-eight times up and fifty-eight times down by the way. In case you hadn't realized. I want to get up to seventy before we run on the track. Then I'm bound to be fastest.

BLIZZARD COMING OVER
THE MOUNTAINS

My grandad nearly won a scholarship to Canada when he was seventeen. We didn't find out until he died. That's how modest he was. He had these old photos in a toffee tin and at the bottom was a bit of newspaper with a black-and-white photo of six runners standing next to a banner saying CANADA CUP FINAL. All the runners are smiling right at the camera and one of them's Grandad. The headline says SIX YOUNG MEN WITH THE WORLD AT THEIR FEET and the writing underneath says *Young runners compete for a scholarship to train in Canada.*

I look at the photo sometimes and wonder who won because, to be honest with you, Grandad looks like the best runner. But he never went to Canada so he must have tripped over his shoelaces or got a fly up his nose or something. Because he was fast. Even when he was old he was fast. It makes me a bit sad, to tell you the truth, because his life might have been easier if he'd lived in a log cabin in the Rocky Mountains.

Anyway, Grandad stayed in east London and worked in the candy factory where he met my nan. She used to roll out the boiled sugar. And they got married and had Mum and Josephine, and when my nan died Grandad brought them up on his own. But he never felt sorry for himself. He was like Mum in that way. He just got on with things.

I've got the newspaper photo in a frame on my bedroom wall next to my Olympic collage. I've got the toffee tin too and Grandad's Olympic ticket and some of his old photos. I keep them under my bed.

And sometimes (and I know this is a bit weird), sometimes I look at the photo and I say, "There's a blizzard coming over the mountains, Grandad. I'm going to get the horses in." I actually say it out loud. And I know that sounds really stupid, but I just think if he's looking at me from the past maybe he'd like to hear that. And anyway I'm going to Canada one day so it might even be true.

OLYMPIC COFFEE

Tyler's standing in the kitchen with a full black garbage bag balanced on his shoulder. Aisha's sort of hanging off him.

"For the worms," she says.

He does this every few months. He brings old coffee from his work cafeteria, the stuff that's been used so there's nothing left but the smell of old boots. Apparently worms love it. I used to think it was left over from the Olympic athletes' coffee and it might have some sort of magic to it and I should have it instead of the worms. But it's just the granules from the security guards and the people who sell the tickets, who might be great runners but probably aren't.

"Any chance of a hand, AJ?" Tyler says. "There's another bag in the car."

I don't want to help because he's not really my favorite person, but it's for Dad so I will, but only after I've ignored him for a few moments. I half nod, half grunt, but I don't move.

"I'll help," says Aisha.

"It's too heavy for you, sweetheart," says Tyler.

Aisha's not bothered though; she heads straight for the front door.

Tyler takes the bag out to Dad in the garden. When he comes back in I jump up so I can get to the front door before him. I don't want to completely wind him up.

The other bag's lying across the backseat of his car. Aisha's prodding it. It's almost as big as she is.

"Leave it, Aisha, will you?" Tyler says.

But Aisha doesn't leave it. She decides to wrestle it onto her shoulder like you might if you had to take a sheep for shearing. Only it's not a sheep.

It's a plastic bag and it splits. Cold wet coffee granules pour all over the seat and trickle onto the curb. Aisha screams.

Tyler pushes past me.

"Thanks for the help, AJ," he says. "Much appreciated."

There's a pulse twitching in his neck.

It takes Tyler and Dad ages to brush the coffee out of the car and shake it out of Aisha's clothes. I try to help but I keep getting in the way. I don't really know what to do with myself.

Dad loads up another bag and carries it into the garden.

Aisha looks up at Tyler. "I'm sorry, Dad," she says.

"Not to worry," says Tyler. "You were trying to help."

I'm sort of standing on the front doorstep wondering whether to go inside when Tyler comes back in. We get caught in the doorway together. His face is pressed right up against mine.

"What's your problem, AJ?" he says.

I can't look at him so I decide to look at the end of my nose and see if I can get it in focus. And I can. I didn't know I could do that.

"My God," Tyler says, and he pushes past.

I feel terrible. I didn't mean for that to happen. I really didn't. If Tyler didn't hate me before, he hates me now. When they leave he can't even look at me. He's that angry.

EMPTY

Me and Mum are making toad-in-the-hole. It's my favorite. Mum lays the sausages in the dish while I beat the batter. I'm best at getting the lumps out. In fact, I pride myself on my lump-free batter. I'm a bit of a natural to tell you the truth. And pancakes, I'm good at those too. I pour the batter over the sausages and they look like big fat worms floating in custard.

"Lovely," says Mum.

We're waiting for the oven to heat up when the lights go out and the oven clicks off. The fridge stops whirring.

"Eddie!" Mum shouts. "The electricity's gone off!"

Dad comes in and takes a flashlight out of his gardening drawer. It's not dark yet but it will be soon.

"The box was beeping," he says.

"We need to put some money in," I say.

We've got a meter box with a slot you put pound coins in to make the electricity work. When it runs out the electricity goes off. Grandad wanted to get us a modern one but Mum likes it. We keep the coins in a jar on the windowsill but there's nothing in the jar.

I open the cupboard under the stairs and check the meter box. The arrow points to Empty. I punch the box in the hope that there's a hidden coin stuck somehow but nothing changes. I feel a little knot in my stomach.

"We'll have to tell Josephine," I say.

"No," says Mum. "She's having a baby."

She's looking at me in that way that says, *Don't you dare*.

"I get paid tomorrow," she says. "I'll ask them to give me some coins."

Her face lights up.

"We can have a picnic."

She gets a tin of baked beans out of the cupboard and we look in the freezer. There's not much there, just ice cream and frozen peas and Dad's pumpkin soup.

"Baked beans and ice cream for tea then," says Mum, "in the garden."

AN ANT OR A SPIDER

We sit on the ground and lean against the wall between the sunflowers. We're wearing coats and we've each got a plastic bowl because you always have a plastic bowl on a picnic. Dad sighs but it's a happy sigh. It's nice out here. He's dotted candles around the garden.

A drop of rain lands on my beans. Not much. The sort of rain you can dodge.

"What do you think gets wettest in the rain?" I say. "An ant or a spider?"

"A spider," says Mum. "The ant can hide under a leaf."

"But if there was no leaf and they were just in a big empty field with a little bit of rain."

"The ant," says Dad. "Spiders run faster."

"Which is it, AJ?" says Mum.

"I don't know."

"You don't know!" she shouts. "Can you find out? I want to know now."

"Probably not," I say.

"A grasshopper can jump around the drops," Dad says.

"Like this," I say.

And suddenly I'm jumping around. And Mum's laughing and Dad gets up and joins in, only he's moving really carefully and I have to make sure I don't crash into him because it's a really small space. It's a bit awkward but he's smiling and Mum's laughing, really screaming. She's like Aisha in that way. When she starts she can't stop.

We stay in the garden until we're cold. Then we go up to bed. We put the candles in the sink to make sure they go out and then we creep upstairs in the dark, feeling the banister all the way up. I quite like it. It's sort of exciting.

"Good night, AJ," Mum says.

"Night, Mum."

"Night, AJ."

"Night, Dad. Thanks for the picnic," I say.

I sleep like a baby. It's really, really nice lying in the dark and thinking about the picnic in the garden and the raindrops landing on the spiders and grasshoppers. It feels like I've been camping. And in the morning we're having canned pineapple.

ALL CORRECT

Miss Charmant runs her finger down the letter with my details on it.

"So it's all correct?" she says.

I nod.

I'm staring at the bit with our address, but letting her think I mean the whole letter. I don't mean the whole letter. I just mean the bit with our address. I don't like lying. That's something I have to tell you about me. I don't lie if I can help it. Sometimes I manage a whole day without lying.

"And if there's a problem we contact your grandad," she says.

She looks at me and smiles. I pretend I've just been turned to stone so I don't have to respond. She doesn't seem to mind.

"Lovely," she says, "thank you."

As I walk away from her desk she says, "Oh, one more thing, AJ."

My heart's racing.

"Yes."

"You're making a very good start here, particularly with your French. Well done."

I'm so relieved the words fall out without me meaning them to.

"*Merci beaucoup*," I say.

(That means *thank you very much* in case you want to know.)

It's embarrassing and I'm hoping no one else heard but Miss Charmant looks pleased.

TEN MILLION KINDS OF BISCUITS

I see Mum before she sees me. She's getting off the bus at the end of our street. She doesn't look happy. You know those ads you get at bus stops where supermarket assistants with shiny teeth smile at the camera to get you to come to the shop like it's a really fun place to be? Well, you wouldn't use a photo of Mum. You can't even see her teeth. She looks so fed up.

Mum's job is filling the biscuit shelves, which might sound easy except there are about ten million kinds of biscuits and they all have to go in the right place. In fact, someone's probably inventing another biscuit at this very moment, and someone else, my mum probably, is going to have to find a space for it. She's okay with that though. She just takes her time. What upsets her is customers getting impatient with her. And that happens a lot.

When I was little Mum worked in the café in our little park. She loved it because usually when people go to a café they're happy. Sometimes I helped. I didn't get paid or anything, but I used to run around and wipe tables and put the paper cups in the trash and fill the fridge with yogurt. I was always hoping someone would knock over a cup of juice or something because then I could clean it up. I loved getting out the bucket and the huge mop with the strings on it and splashing around. I probably showed off a bit. I used to march around and talk really loudly and even though I sort of hated myself for it I couldn't stop. And the more I hated myself the louder I got. Sometimes I'd think, *Shut up, AJ!* but it didn't make any difference. It was a pretty nice place to work actually.

And the time I liked most was winter when there was almost no one there—just Mum and me and this woman with big hoop earrings who ran the café. I especially liked it when the crossing guard came in for a cup of tea. It's like when you're small you can't really imagine people anywhere else except where you usually see them. She used to lean her stop sign against the window. She didn't come in the summer. She probably couldn't stand to see all the little kids again.

When the café closed it took Mum ages to find the supermarket job so she doesn't complain. She just comes home with that little cloud over her head.

I wait for her to see me and when she does she waves and the cloud vanishes.

BEST SOUND IN THE WORLD

Coins falling into a meter must be one of the best sounds in the world. Like water dripping through the rain forest or the screech of a hawk in the desert. Mum's got a bag of coins from work and I slot them all in and turn the creaky handle. They drop into the box and the lights go back on. The oven flashes and the fridge begins to whirr. We're all smiling.

Mum takes the toad-in-the-hole out of the fridge and slides it into the trash. She doesn't like to take chances. Dad puts some spinach and potatoes on the table.

"Soup," he says.

"And cake," says Mum.

I know it will be ages until dinner's ready because Mum and Dad are extra-careful. Even though they know the recipes off by heart they always check. Grandad made recipe sheets with pictures and put stickers on cups so they can measure things out, and colors on the oven dials so Mum knows what temperature to use. He was good like that. Most people wouldn't even think of that sort of thing. And anyway I don't mind waiting. I've got training to do.

"Do you mind if I run on the stairs?" I say.

Mum rolls her eyes.

"We're running on the track tomorrow. I need to get some practice."

"Can't you go to the park?" she says.

"It shuts soon," I say. "And I don't want to miss dinner."

(Neither of these things are lies.)

Mum smiles. She doesn't really mind. The fridge is whirring and she's about to make a cake.

"Go on then," she says. "But hurry up."

I run up and down the stairs seventy-two times really, really fast. By the time I get to the seventieth run I can hardly breathe but I keep going until I reach seventy-two because that's how old Grandad was and that feels lucky. That's up *and* down the stairs by the way. Seventy-two times up and seventy-two times down the stairs.

RUNNING ON EMPTY

My luckiest thing is my Olympic collage. It's got my ticket in it, three photos of Usain Bolt, and a photo of me, Mum, Dad, and Grandad in a crowd of people outside the stadium after the race. You could say we're standing in the crowd but we're not exactly. It's more that we're trying not to fall over because everyone behind us is pushing and waving their flags, like they want to be in the world's biggest selfie. Grandad's sort of holding Dad up and Mum's waving her flag and screaming. You can't really see my face because I'm looking up at Mum. Grandad put all the photos in a frame for me. It's the best thing ever.

I touch the frame before I set off for school. I did that before we scattered Grandad's ashes (to make sure they were him I suppose) and I do it this morning because we're running on the track. Not that I need any luck, but I suppose you can't have too much. My running shoes are hard and squashed because I haven't worn them for eight weeks and there's rubber hanging off the soles, but you know what—they're the best running shoes I've ever had. Grandad got them for me so that's even more luck.

I have an extra slice of toast for breakfast because Grandad always said you shouldn't run on empty. He said to think of yourself like an engine— you need a full tank. As I walk out of the house I feel like a machine. Invincible.

Crystal's waiting for me at the school gate. I've got my PE bag balanced on my head. Don't ask me why.

"Aw, AJ," she says, "are you excited?"

I'm trying not to smile.

"Do you think there might be someone faster than you?" she says.

"I dunno," I say. "Amit could beat me."

(I'm trying not to smirk. I'm sure he won't.)

"Oh yeah... ," says Crystal.

I'm not sure if she doesn't believe it or if she's still thinking about what I said about running faster than Usain Bolt.

A THOUSAND PERCENT

The changing room stinks of deodorant. Loads of boys are spraying it around to make themselves smell better. I wish I had some but I've got one of those sticks with a rollerball. I don't bring it to school. It's embarrassing.

Amit's wearing new running shoes and jogging on the spot. I know mine look rubbish but I don't care. You should see me run in them, that is if you can focus. I put my gym clothes on and glance at myself in the mirror. I look sort of okay. Everyone's going to be amazed. Then I get out my shoes and put one foot in. At first I think there's an old sock inside but when I put my hand in there's nothing there.

Mr. Higgins comes in.

"Come on, lads, hurry up."

I pull my sock up as high as I can to thin it out and try again, but it's no better. And then I realize: My shoes don't fit! My left shoe is just about okay, but my right shoe is at least a size too small. It was tight before but now I can't actually get my foot flat on the floor. I feel sick.

Mr. Higgins is pacing up and down the changing room.

"Come on," he says. "Show some effort. Wake up, wake up."

I'm putting my school shoes back on when he looms over me.

"Running shoes!" he yells. "I want to see you in running shoes!"

He doesn't look like he wants me to explain. I put my running shoes back on and as the boys file out I hobble behind them.

Mr. Higgins is full of testosterone, that hormone that makes boys grow into men. It's bursting out of him. It's in his hair and all over his skin. He probably has to wash it off every night or he'd turn into a gorilla. Out by the track, some of the boys are talking, some are warming up.

"Right, now let's see what you can do. Around the track, please."

"Aw," someone says.

"Twice."

He blows his whistle.

Amit's of course in front straightaway. That's what he's like. He's such a show-off. He can't just hold back for a while and then shoot ahead; he has to show everyone right from the beginning that he can take the lead. Not like me: I hold back and then sprint at the end. Anyway, I'm with him just about but it feels terrible. My feet are in agony. I'm sort of running and sort of limping and then Amit leaves me behind and the other boys are overtaking me, even the boys who don't care.

It's just me now, and Harvey, who's chewing gum and chatting all the way around, even if nobody's listening. I can't run anymore so I'm sort of walking. I'm trying not to cry.

"I hate this, don't you?" Harvey says. "I hate it so much."

He spits his gum onto the track.

"Don't do that!"

"Sorreee."

He doesn't pick it up. I can't believe it. Someone will run around and it'll stick to his shoe.

"It's actually bad for you, running," he says. "It jiggles all your organs around. Your heart and kidneys and all that. I read it on the Internet. Sometimes they even come undone."

Is he serious?!

"What do you mean, 'come undone'?"

"Well," he says, "they sort of undo. So you might suddenly find that your heart isn't attached to your—"

"Your what?"

He's really annoying.

"You know. Whatever it's attached to. What's the heart attached to?"

"I dunno."

(Actually I don't know. What is the heart attached to?)

"It's attached to everything!" he says at last. "It's like the boiler's attached to all the taps so things keep working and if the boiler breaks down you don't get any hot water. Well, you might suddenly find your heart isn't attached to anything. It's just floating around your body. And then you drop down dead."

I'm nodding but I'm thinking, *What an idiot.*

"So running's not natural. Do you think cavemen ran around a track? Nooooo. They'd do a little bit of fishing or hunting and then they'd stop and eat some berries. It's bad for you a hundred percent. And football's even worse. All that stop-starting. What's the point of that?"

He stops to watch the other runners. They're about to lap us.

"A thousand percent bad for you actually," he says, in case I didn't get it.

"Come on, you two." Mr. Higgins is shouting at us.

I feel terrible. Amit's lapped me. He's right out in the lead. He glances back at me. I can't tell if he's smiling or frowning.

"Teacher's pets," says Harvey.

It takes me and Harvey ages to get around the track once. Mr. Higgins comes up at the beginning of the second lap and says, "Run or else you'll be doing it after school." Then he sticks with us. He doesn't just run beside us, he touches his toes and spins around and runs backward like he's doing a lap of honor. All the other boys have finished. They're high-fiving or looking tired and they're half watching us. No matter how bad they feel, looking at us is making them feel better. Some of them are laughing.

As we reach the finish line Harvey overtakes me! Then he collapses on the ground, very dramatic.

"Argh, argh. I'm not built for this, sir," he says. "It's bad for you, you know."

Everyone's laughing. Me, I can't make everyone laugh. I stand really still and stare at my feet. I feel so bad.

Amit's beaming. Mr. Higgins has actually got his

hand on Amit's shoulder. He's probably passing on some of his testosterone.

"Well done, lad."

Then he turns to me.

"What's your name?"

"AJ."

He hates me already.

"Well, AJ," he says. "You don't have to steam ahead like Amit here but you do have to try. Next week I'd like to see more effort."

I'm so embarrassed. I can see the shape of my toes though my shoes.

"STRIVE," he says. "Strength, tenacity, rigor, impetus, values, energy."

It's a rubbish slogan. He probably made it up himself.

"Whatever," I say when I'm sure he can't hear me.

SORT-OF-SORRY FACE

Crystal catches me as I walk out of school. I'm trying not to limp.

"How was the race?" she says.

"Rubbish."

"What happened?"

"My shoes don't fit."

"Tell your mum," she says.

I shake my head.

"Tell the school then."

"Duh," I say. "Schools don't buy shoes for kids."

(I'm being horrible and I can't help it.)

Crystal makes a sort-of-sorry face. It's the same face I make when she tells me how her dad never stops talking.

"Don't worry," she says. "I've got five pounds. We'll get some from Easy Exchange."

IDIOT

Aisha's standing at her school gate with a group of kids and her face says, *Something's happened*. She's holding a paper plate.

"What's up?" I say.

"It's those boys," she says. "I just threw cake at them. They said I look like a frog."

I look at the boys. There's five of them and they're about eight years old and they're all carrying slices of cake on paper plates. One boy's got cake in his hair.

"Idiots," I say.

"They're not idiots," she says. "They're just quite annoying."

She's being quite annoying herself.

We start walking only she's not in any sort of hurry. She keeps looking back at them. She might as well say, *Nah-nah-nah-nah-nah-nah*.

"Can you just ignore them, please?"

She puts her nose in the air, walks a few steps, and then turns around.

"He's my cousin," she yells. "He's at secondary school."

"That's not ignoring them," I say. "That's winding them up."

The first bit of cake hits Aisha on the back of the head. Then they come from all directions. I don't see the jam sponge until it lands in my face. I'm spinning around and around.

Aisha's shouting, "I hate you, I hate you," but she looks like she's trying not to smile. She's covered in cake. So am I. A group of little kids run over and suddenly Aisha's beaming. She's the center of attention.

It is so embarrassing. I sometimes think if Aisha was my age she'd be my best friend and sometimes I wish I didn't know her at all. She's becoming a liability.

I feel ridiculous and I look ridiculous. She doesn't. She looks like a Year 4 kid who's been in a cake fight with her friends. I look like a secondary-school kid who's been in a cake fight with some Year 4s.

As if things can't get any worse we pass Amit leaning on the bus stop. He doesn't say anything but I know what he's thinking. He's thinking, *What an idiot*.

I don't talk to Aisha the whole way home. I march ahead while she skips behind me. Every now and then she does a cartwheel. When we get home we hardly speak, except Aisha hums the whole time like she's had the best day ever. As soon she's gone I jump in the bath. My toes are red and shiny and the skin's peeled off. I hold my feet under the cold tap until they're numb.

I come out of the bathroom just as Mum gets in.

"AJ," she says, "you've had a bath!"

She's delighted. I can't look at her.

BALLOONS

Sometimes I get this horrible feeling that my dreams are never going to come true. And today's one of those days. Because every day another dream is gone. It's like there's a whole line of balloons filled with helium so they're bouncing and bouncing and each one is one of my dreams and they go on and on forever into the distance. And they just keep popping.

Like when I was five, me and Crystal wanted to build a trampoline so big you could bounce all the way up to the moon, and then someone told us that if you get to the moon there's no oxygen so you'd die, so that was one balloon burst.

And then when I was eight I really wanted to be on the school football team, even though I don't like football. I just wanted to hang out with those kids and be popular but I never got onto the team. Even when a vomiting bug was going around the school and that was my big chance I only got to be a sub and they never called me on. So that was another balloon gone because I never did get to be on the team and win the cup and stand up in assembly to show off my medal.

And when I was ten Amit had a climbing-wall party and I really wanted to go because I'd never been. So I went up to him at recess and asked if I could go (it must have been really embarrassing) and he said he could only take five kids but if someone dropped out I could take their place. And I was hoping someone would be ill or fall out of a tree and break their arm and then I could go. But no one dropped out and that was another balloon burst and then later I realized probably Amit was never going to invite me anyway so that was another one.

And loads and loads of my dreams burst when Grandad died because I had wanted to do so many things with him. It's like all I could hear was *pop pop pop*. I could hardly hear anything else except for the sound of balloons bursting. And the trouble is I can still see balloons going right off into the distance and they're really bright and all different colors and they're just bobbing there waiting to be popped.

I talked to Crystal about it once but she didn't get it. Because things usually work out for her and everyone likes her.

STUFF

I couldn't really concentrate at Grandad's funeral. It was held one week after he died and it just felt so weird because everyone kept talking about him as if he was there but he wasn't. I couldn't really make any sense of the world after he died because he wasn't in it anymore.

Mum and Josephine said no black so everyone looked like they were at a wedding—except the flowers had *Forever in our thoughts* written on them and *Deepest sympathy*. It was like when Josephine and Tyler got married and all I was really thinking about was the food and not spoiling my suit, and not letting Mum lose her hat. And the funeral was the same, except the tears were different and I've grown out of my suit so I wore shorts and a T-shirt. But I did keep thinking about Mum's hat because she wore the same one. It's pink with a sort of net on it. I was hoping after Josephine and Tyler got married I'd never have to worry about that hat again but there I was, looking across the church and seeing it on an empty pew or on the table in the hall next to the spilled lemonade. But I felt no emotion at all. In fact, worrying about Mum's hat gave me something to think about.

Later Josephine said to me, after the funeral I mean, not after the wedding, she said, "AJ, what are you thinking?"

And I shrugged.

She said, "Does that mean nothing?"

And I nodded.

She said, "Sometimes nothing can be very full of stuff."

And she smiled. And her makeup had run so her eyes looked very small and pink. Like a mouse. Because of course Grandad was her dad.

So I said he felt a bit like he was my dad too and she nodded.

"He felt a bit like you were his son," she said.

And apart from that I didn't talk to anyone. I just held on to Mum's hat and afterward I took Aisha across the road to the swings and pushed her and listened to her sing something from *Frozen*. She gets over things pretty quick.

But Josephine was right. Nothing can hold a lot

of stuff. Because the empty space where Grandad was is overflowing now. It's like he used to just be in one place and now he's everywhere.

ASTEROID

The best way to do a boring job is to pretend you're doing something else. That's what I've found anyway. So if I'm replacing a fuse in a fuse box I pretend I'm defusing a bomb and if I'm changing a lightbulb I pretend I invented electricity and I'm showing it off for the first time. I imagine a little round of applause when the light goes on.

And on Saturdays I tell myself if I don't get my chores done by midday an asteroid will land on our house. And the first thing I think of when I wake up is an asteroid speeding right toward me. It gets me out of bed, I can tell you that.

So I'm whizzing around, putting out the rubbish, sorting the washing, wiping, and vacuuming, and all the time I'm watching the clock tick closer to midday. Mum gets quite annoyed because she and Dad like to chat and drink tea while they do their chores and it's probably quite stressful having me jumping around like the house is on fire (which it nearly is). I don't think she'd mind if she knew I was saving the world from an asteroid.

I finish at 11:28 and the asteroid flies off in another direction. Mum wants me to get some milk from the convenience store so I race down the street. I have to calm down before I go in, in case the girl's there. I don't want to look like an idiot.

An old woman in a sari, who might be her nan, is sitting on a stool just inside the door. She nods when I go in. And then I see the girl. She's behind the counter and the stupid thing is as soon as I see her I can't remember what I came for. It's like my brain leaves my body. I walk down the aisle staring at the soups and the tins of beans and the newspapers and the birthday cards and my mind goes completely blank.

A man comes in all smiles. He looks like he's been jogging. He picks up a newspaper and a carton of milk and bounces to the counter. I grab a carton of milk and follow him.

"Do you have any bread rolls left?" he says.

They get these really nice rolls in on Saturday mornings. They're soft and dusted with flour. Mum likes the way the flour falls onto her plate but they're usually sold out when I get there.

"Sorry," the girl says, "all gone."

The man doesn't seem to mind. He chats to her about the weather and how he has to pick up his son from football and he's glad it's not raining. It's sort of hard to believe. He's talking to her like she's a normal person. Like he's not completely amazed by her eyes (which are hazel, by the way, with the longest lashes I've ever seen).

When he's gone I put the milk on the counter

and sort of grunt. I can't quite look at her. She's too perfect. Her hair hangs over her shoulder in a thick black braid. She gives me my change and sort of smiles. I don't even grunt this time. I just scuttle out. It doesn't matter though. Not really. It's enough just to know that at this moment at this time in the history of the world we're standing in the same space, breathing the same air.

EASY EXCHANGE

Crystal's waiting outside Easy Exchange.

"I can't stay long," she says, "we've got visitors." She rolls her eyes. "My dad's going to be so embarrassing."

I've only met Crystal's dad a few times but I have to tell you if you see him coming you should walk away because he never stops talking. And it's not funny stuff or interesting stuff. It's just stuff that pours out of his head. And the worst thing is, if Crystal tells him anything interesting (and she knows loads of interesting things) he always thinks he knows better.

I give her a sort-of-sorry face like she gave me about my shoes.

"Come on then," she says.

Easy Exchange, if you've never been, is one of those shops where if you need money you take your stuff in and they give you cash. Like if my dad didn't want his wormery we could take that in and they'd buy it. Except I suppose they probably wouldn't. They only buy stuff they can sell. But you know what I mean.

I look in the window. There's all this stuff that people took into the shop but maybe didn't really want to sell. It makes me feel bad before we've even gone in.

"Do we have to buy them from here?" I say.

Crystal gives me a look.

"We've got five pounds, remember," she says.

There's computer games and electrical stuff and musical instruments and jewelry and even a lawn mower but there's no shoes and no running shoes. Nothing you'd put on your feet in fact. Not even a pair of slippers. It's depressing. Crystal goes to ask the salesperson and comes back shaking her head.

"You know what?" I say. "It doesn't matter."

I'm trying to look like I'm not at all bothered but I can't seem to smile.

When we get outside Crystal tries to give me the five pounds.

"You might see something," she says. "You never know."

I do know but I don't say. I just shake my head.

"No thanks," I say. "I'm all right."

AN ANGEL

I run to the shopping center as fast as I can. I want to be surrounded by shiny new stuff. I'm wearing my school shoes and they're rubbish for running but I'm still pretty fast. At the entrance a man dressed as a rabbit tries to hand me a leaflet. When I don't take it he does a sort of bunny hop behind me. It's embarrassing. I speed-walk away. You can't run in a shopping center. People think you've been shoplifting.

I'm walking past the Choc Box when a message jumps out at me: KEEP RUNNING, AJ. At first I keep walking with the scowl on my face that says *I hate chocolate* (even though I love it). But then I'm sort of looking at the image in my head—like it's stuck to my eyeballs—and I'm thinking, *It did say "Keep running, AJ." I'm sure it did.* So I walk back and in the window there's a pile of broken chocolate and right at the front is a chocolate running shoe with KEEP RUNNING, AJ written on it in white icing. And above the pile a sign says 99P SALE.

I stare at the shoe for ages and I don't know what to do because somewhere at the back of my mind I'm thinking, *Grandad ordered that for me.* And I can feel my heart breaking—honestly, it feels like it's folding in half—because who else would do that for me? And he didn't live long enough to pick it up.

I shake out my pockets even though I know they're empty. I wish I'd taken Crystal's money. I scour the ground in case someone's dropped a pound coin but there's none. I never noticed how clean it is in here before. They probably have loads of cleaners who find all the small change when they're picking up the burger bags.

I'm in a sweat now. A little boy's pointing at the shoe. He wants it but it's got my name on it. And suddenly I have a really awful feeling that life is so unfair and I have to do something really embarrassing to make it better. I walk up to a man pushing an old woman in a wheelchair, thinking he might be kind.

"Could I have some money for a cup of tea?" I mumble.

The man's eyes narrow.

"Shouldn't you be at school?" he says.

"It's Saturday," I say.

He swerves the wheelchair past me.

"I'll call security," he says.

And then I see this woman and even though she's on her own she's smiling. She's wearing a beanie and dark curls spill out around her face. I walk over to her.

"I'm really sorry," I say, "but I need to buy that chocolate shoe. It's got my name on it."

She comes to the shop with me and looks in the window.

"Okay," she says.

She's carrying an artist's portfolio and she puts it down between her feet, takes a purse out of her pocket, and dips her fingers in. She's got blue and green paint on her hands.

"Let's see if I've got the change," she says.

Then she counts out one 50-pence coin, two 20 pence, one 5 pence, and two 2 pences and drops them into my hand.

"There you go," she says.

"Thank you."

"You're welcome."

And in that minute she's the most beautiful person in the world. She's like an angel. And she doesn't even wait for me to buy the shoe. She just picks up her portfolio and walks off and she doesn't turn around to check that I go into the shop. She trusts that I'll get the shoe and maybe if I don't she doesn't want to know.

The shop salesperson asks if I want her to peel the message off.

"No," I say. "It's for me. I'm AJ."

"You should probably pay the full price then," she says.

I give her my death stare. If she was younger she might make a fuss but she can't be bothered. When I walk out with the shoe I don't know whether to laugh or cry. But by the time I get home I'm sort of bouncing because it feels like a good sign. Things are going to get better.

PERFECT

Mum's so surprised when she sees the chocolate running shoe. I tell her the story (skipping the bit about the begging). It's not lying. It's just not telling the full truth. Her face goes soft and sad.

"Aw, AJ," she says, "your grandad must have done that."

When Dad sees it he sort of shudders.

"Isn't that nice?" Mum says. "Grandad did it."

Dad looks upset. He goes into the garden and stands there looking at the sunflowers. I know how he feels. It's confusing to have the chocolate shoe when Grandad's not here to give it to us.

It seems a shame to eat the chocolate. It's so smooth and perfect, but me and Mum break off small bits. It should be delicious but it isn't.

SEVENTY-FIVE TIMES

I run up and down the stairs seventy-five times. It feels like a good number. I'm not going to stop training, in case you're wondering. I'm bound to get some running shoes one day. I'm just bound to. That's seventy-five times up the stairs and seventy-five times down by the way. My feet are still sore and I'm wearing out my socks but I keep going anyway. Grandad would smile if he could see me. I think he'd be proud.

When I finish I sit on the bottom stair until I get my breath back and try not to think about the next PE class and what I'm going to do then. Instead I talk to myself in French, because I don't know many French words so I can only think about my favorite food (*poisson et frites*), my favorite color (*vert*) and the place where I live (*une petite maison à Londres*). That's fish and chips, green, and a little house in London.

A CHOCOLATE HORSE

Aisha's at our house. She's trying to draw a horse but it looks like a dog in a wig. The chocolate shoe's on the table.

"Why did you get chocolate and I didn't?" she says.

"Well, I was starting secondary school. You would have got one then."

"But I won't now, will I?" she says. "Because Grandad's dead."

"Well," I say, "someone else might get you one."

"Okay," she says, "I'll remind you."

Then she squeals. She really does squeal. She's like that. I'd like to say I used to be like that but I don't think I was ever was.

"Grandad bought you a present and then he died but you still got it! It's like magic!" she says.

She laughs for a moment and then stops herself. "Is that sad?"

"Not really," I say.

She breaks off a chunk of chocolate and shoves it into her mouth.

"Mmm," she says, "delicious."

Then she takes some more.

"If ever you want to get me a surprise, you can

get me a chocolate horse," she says. "Or even a real horse. Do you think they do chocolate horses?"

"Maybe," I say.

"Will you get me one?"

"Okay," I say, "I'll try to do that before I die."

She takes another bit of chocolate and gets back to her drawing. I'm going to hide it when she's gone or she'll finish it off. She's not really giving it the appreciation it deserves.

PEANUT-BUTTER-AND-ORANGE BISCUITS

When Mum gets in from work she looks like she's going to cry. And that's a bad thing because the only times I've seen Mum cry were at Grandad's funeral and when we scattered his ashes.

"Some people asked me for peanut-butter-and-orange biscuits," she says, "and I couldn't find them. They were laughing at me."

"Sounds revolting," I say.

"Yes, but they didn't mean that," Mum says. "They were looking for a jar of peanut butter and they were looking for orange biscuits."

I feel so sorry for her. She's been surrounded by impatient people all her life. I never even realized it when I was small. I just thought there were loads of bad-tempered people in the world because there was always someone behind us tutting or rolling their eyes. It gets me down a bit if you want to know the truth. I have to stop myself from getting annoyed about it or I'd become one of those angry people too.

"Well," says Aisha, "I think it sounds like a lovely biscuit! It's the best invention ever!"

Mum smiles.

"In fact," says Aisha, "if someone asked me, I'd think it was a biscuit too."

ALPHABET SOUP

My parents don't mean to be embarrassing. They don't want to control me or stop me from doing things. They just want to be kind. Lots of kids are beginning to hate their parents because the parents try to control them. They get all worked up about stuff because their kids aren't cute anymore and then their parents don't think they're wonderful and the kids can see as clear as day that their parents aren't wonderful either.

Crystal's just realized her dad is really, really boring. When she was young she thought he was fascinating but now she says his mouth's too full of words. She says it's like alphabet soup: the words just go on and on and half the time they don't make any sense. She says when they're eating around the table and her dad's talking everyone else in her family is choking on their yawns. Their faces twist with trying to keep the yawn inside. What they really want to do is close their eyes and let their heads slump onto their plates. She says it's embarrassing. Even just in the family. Because her dad thinks he's really interesting and he's not.

Crystal says one day she's going to close her eyes and let her head drop right onto her plate and when she does she knows she'll be free. She might do it the day she leaves home. Maybe at breakfast.

Alphabet soup, by the way, used to be my favorite, even though now I know it tastes revolting. It's one of those things you don't realize until you're older. I used to think it was great to be eating letters. Grandad got it for me. I'm going to buy it one day. Just to remind myself how you can be tricked into thinking something's great when really the thing you're excited about is something pretty rubbish. Like if you took all the excitement away you'd see it's soggy pasta.

GRAY

We're running on the track again tomorrow. Well, Amit is. I'll be limping around with Harvey I suppose. I can't sleep for thinking about it because I've always been a good runner, it's always been my thing, and now I haven't got a thing. And even though I can run seventy-five times up and down the stairs that doesn't really count for anything. Not in the real world.

I get out of bed and go down to the kitchen. It's nearly midnight. Dad's in the garden. He's got his coat on over his pajamas and his hat pulled down over his ears and he's walking up and down. When he sees me he comes in.

"AJ," he says.

There are dark circles around his eyes.

"I couldn't sleep," I say.

"Cup of tea?"

I nod.

A cat leaps onto the window ledge and stares in at us. Its eyes are shining.

"You must miss Grandad," Dad says.

I nod.

"You must miss him too."

Dad nods.

We drink our tea and as we do I notice a bit of hair sticking out from under Dad's hat and it's going gray. And I haven't seen that before.

DYING INSECTS

I've padded my toes with toilet paper and cut my toenails and slit the toe of my shoes so I've got more room. They don't exactly feel better. They just rub in different places.

As I stumble onto the field Mr. Higgins calls me over.

"A bit more effort this time please, AJ," he says.

I can't quite look in his eyes and I don't want to look at my feet in case he does too so I imagine a little bird on his shoulder pecking at his ear and stare at that.

The run goes even worse than I thought it would. Amit streaks ahead and I try to run but can't so I end up walking with Harvey. Just before we reach the finish Harvey lies down on the grass. I can't believe it. If he rolled a few times he'd be over the line.

"Pity it's not snowing," he says, "we could make snow angels."

It feels like the ultimate humiliation to beat Harvey at the finish, like the only person I can beat is someone lying on the grass, so without really thinking I lie down too.

Harvey's got his arms and legs in the air and he's wriggling. He looks like a dying insect who just needs someone to come along and flip him over so he can scuttle off under a leaf.

Mr. Higgins runs over. He's shouting.

"Get up, boys. Get up!"

I put my legs and arms in the air and do the insect wriggle. It seems like the only thing I can do. Maybe everyone will forget I can't run. Maybe everyone will think I'm funny. And the finish line is so close. The other boys are laughing and I'm laughing too and I feel good. Sort of. I think. Mr. Higgins stares at my feet. He looks disgusted.

When Mr. Higgins has given everyone their pep talk he turns to me and Harvey.

"What was that all about then, lads?" he says. "What was the point?"

"Sorry, sir," says Harvey. "I'll try harder next time."

He's beaming in a sort of charming way.

Mr. Higgins looks at me.

"And you?"

I shrug.

"Your attitude is terrible," he says.

Out of the corner of my eye I can see Amit watching. I'm dying inside. I can't say I'll do better next time because I can't. I can hardly walk.

"Whatever," I say.

(I actually say *whatever*!)

"Okay," he says, "my classroom after school."

ONE HUNDRED LINES

Mr. Higgins is waiting at his desk when I come in. He looks so smug. I hate him.

"Sit down," he says, and points to a table with some lined paper and a pen on it.

I sit down.

"Right," he says, "one hundred lines."

What is this? It's like the olden days! Is he really allowed to do this? He points at the whiteboard.

"Write that down one hundred times. I've got marking to do so we can keep each other company."

I can't believe it. He's put random letters on the

whiteboard just to make it more difficult. It says ODLLIWYRROSEMITTXEN.

"Just write it," he says.

He doesn't even bother catching my eye after that. He just does his paperwork, whatever it is that PE teachers do.

I always thought if I ever got lines I'd write them a word at a time down the page. But I can't do that. I write a hundred *o*'s down the side of three pages. By the end they look like flat balloons. I put smiley faces in a couple of them and then a few sad ones and then I catch myself and stop.

Then I do a hundred *d*'s and then the *ll*'s and right though the letters until I get to *rose* and *mitt* and *xen*, which are easier. And all the time I'm wondering what Grandad would say if he could see me and I just don't know.

Crystal appears at the window. She's mouthing, *What are you doing?* I point at my page and she winks and ducks down. Then she's gone.

I can see Aisha in her playground with a whole lot of little kids who are staying at the after-school club. They're playing some game with hula hoops. There's a woman in a tracksuit demonstrating what to do and every time Aisha gets the hula hoop over her head she's so proud it's almost like she lifts off the ground. I can tell her a mile off. It's funny you can recognize someone just by their walk. Aisha's walk is sort of hopeful. She's like a balloon on a string, a balloon with helium in it. If you let go, she'd go right up into the sky. I can imagine her bouncing into the clouds and not coming down again. She's sort of doing that on the field. She seems to jump higher than everyone else.

"Can you crack on?" Mr. Higgins says. "I'd quite like to get home before Christmas."

"Me too," I say.

My stomach's rumbling. I'm really hungry. I think about not doing all the lines properly just to get back at him but then he might give me another hundred, so when I've finished I check them. Then I hold up the sheets of paper. The whole thing takes ages.

Mr Higgins doesn't even look at them.

"Okay. Now write it the other way around."

"What?"

"Back to front."

My mouth falls open.

"Just once."

So I do and as I do they turn into a sentence:

Next time sorry will do.

He's looking at me now and I'm staring back.

"Sorry," I say.

"Off you go."

I don't know if I'm angry or if I want to cry. All I know is I feel rubbish.

CHOKING HORSE

Mum drops a slice of bread in the toaster when she hears me come in.

"Boys," she says, "always hungry."

Then she fills the kettle.

It's hard to explain how I go from feeling rubbish but just about okay to feeling furious but that's what happens. I look at the teapot and the toaster and I know the toaster's about to set off the smoke alarm and suddenly I hate everything. I pick up the teapot and throw it.

I'm sorry even before it hits the floor. It smashes into loads of pieces. I turn around and see Dad standing in the doorway with his hand over his mouth. I don't look long enough to catch his eyes. I run straight out the front door and slam it behind me and as I do I hear Mum shout, "I'm sorry, AJ, I'm sorry." And then the smoke alarm goes off.

And the awful thing is I didn't have to do it. Because before I threw the teapot I shook it to check there was no tea in it because I didn't want tea to go everywhere. So I can't even say I wasn't in control.

As I run down the street this awful noise comes out of me like a choking horse and I can't stop it and I don't even care. I race past Grandad's house, turn the corner, and run down the street, past the row of shops (I pick up speed when I get to the convenience store so I do care a little), and then to the park. When I get there I run around and around and around the path, not looking at the red dots, until the *thud* of my feet makes my head feel completely empty and I'm thinking nothing at all. My shoes are slipping and my feet are hurting but I never want to stop running because when I'm running I'm somewhere else.

When I can't run any farther I walk slowly out of the park, trying to get my breath back. Victor waves me over.

"You run like your grandad used to," he says. "Just like him."

"What do you mean?"

"Like a boy with a lot of life ahead of him," he says.

I don't know what to say so I grunt and walk on. I think of Grandad as a boy with a lot of life ahead and it makes me feel terrible. Because he never went anywhere in his life. He could have lived in the Rocky Mountains but he couldn't even win the race.

SORRY

Mum and Dad are standing exactly where I left them. They look like they haven't moved, except they've cleared up the teapot. It's like someone's waved a magic wand to tidy up the mess and left them standing where they were.

"I'm sorry," I say.

"I'm sorry too," says Mum.

"You didn't do anything wrong," I say. "It was all my fault."

She shrugs.

"I know I'm annoying."

I give her a hug. It's all I can do. I can't bring the teapot back but maybe I can get rid of the angry boy who broke her favorite thing. We sit at the table together while Dad heats some soup. And when it gets dark he lights some candles in the garden. Maybe in case the electricity runs out or maybe just because they're pretty. And the electricity doesn't go out and the candles do look pretty.

SECOND SKIN

When I was two I always wore my Wellington boots. I wouldn't take them off. I even wore them to bed and Mum would have to pull them off when I was asleep. I never wanted to let them go. They made me feel safe. I was like that about other things too, especially dressing-up costumes. One summer I had a Spider-Man outfit and nothing would get me out of it. It just made me feel good.

And one time, when my grandad was taking me to see Josephine, I put on my diving kit—my wet suit, goggles, and flippers, the whole lot. The ones that someone gave me for dressing up and I never actually went in the water with. And I sat like that in the back of the car and I even had the snorkel in my mouth for the whole journey. It must have been really embarrassing. But I just needed it to get through. I can't explain except to say it was like a second skin. And now I could really do with a second skin.

STARDUST

We are all made of stardust. So we never exactly disappear. We just become stardust again. I tell Aisha this and she likes it. I start to tell her about stars being fireballs made of all the different parts in the universe.

"There's new stars being created in the universe all the time," I say, "even now."

She's not really that interested in the science of it.

"So if we're all made of stardust, does that mean I'm a star?" she says.

She's dancing around now.

"Like on *The X Factor*?"

She's doing a floppy thing with her hands and she's kicking her feet and she's a bundle of pure happiness. She looks like she's made of rubber and I know if she was on TV the whole crowd would be on their feet and cheering.

"Yes, like *The X Factor*," I say.

"Like Grandad?"

"Like Grandad."

"Because even though he's dead he's still stardust?"

I nod.

"And like you?"

My eyes are getting wet and I don't even know why. I'm nodding like one of those dogs people have in their cars. I'm nodding like a nodding dog so she won't see I'm trying not to cry.

She dances over and takes my hands.

"Like you," she says. "You're a star too. Even though you're at a difficult age." She screws up her nose and laughs. "You're still a star."

Her eyes are shining and she looks like she's just arrived on this planet, which I suppose she has.

PARENTS EVENING

I tell Mum and Dad about parents evening an hour before it starts. They stare at each other for ages. They look like the roof's blown off the house and it's about to rain.

At last Dad says, "I can't go, AJ. I'm sorry. I can't go."

"Don't worry, I'll go on my own," I say.

I don't really want either of them to come. It'd be embarrassing for all of us.

"No you won't," Mum says.

"Why not?"

"Because you've got to go with a guardian. So I'm coming."

She's half smiling, half ferocious. Her face says she won't take no for an answer.

"It'll be all right," she says. "I'll just keep my mouth shut. Not a word."

She puts her finger to her lips.

By the time we get to school the hall's packed. Mum hesitates as we walk in. I don't know how she looks to other people but to me she looks scared. I'd normally put my arm through hers but I can't quite do it here.

It's so crowded you can't really see who's with who, except that sometimes I see a parent who looks like a kid in my class, just older. It's weird. Crystal's mum looks just like Crystal except Crystal straightens her hair. Her dad's wearing too much hair gel and talking in a really loud voice. Crystal's staring at the floor.

Amit's with his mum. He doesn't seem to be embarrassed by her but I know I would be. She keeps waving at people across the room.

But apart from Amit's mum I bet that most of the people in the room wish they were somewhere else. I bet even the teachers don't want to be here. I bet they can't wait to go home.

We see my English teacher first. She jumps up and shakes Mum's hand.

"Pleased to meet you," she says.

Mum smiles and my teacher tells her I'm good at writing stories and I need to improve my spelling and put my hand up a bit more.

Then we go to Math, Geography, Science, History, IT. We've got a little map and we're racing through. No one says anything really bad about me and Mum says nothing at all except when we're on our own.

"Am I doing all right?" Mum says.

"You're fine," I say. "Only French and PE to go."

"I won't say anything," she says. "Keep my mouth shut. That's the best idea."

"You can talk if you like," I say. "If you want to say something, you can."

She shakes her head and runs her finger over her mouth.

"Not a word," she says. "They'll think I'm stupid."

French goes well too. Miss Charmant says, "*Bonsoir*, AJ," and I reply, "*Bonsoir*, Mademoiselle Charmant." It's embarrassing but Mum and Miss Charmant look proud. Miss Charmant says to keep working hard.

Then she says to Mum, "Do you have any questions?"

Mum looks at me in horror. Then she shakes her head.

"Well," says Miss Charmant, "lovely to meet you."

Mum smiles.

She's still smiling when we get to Mr. Higgins. He's leaning back in his chair, one foot on the desk, the other on the floor. He can't just sit like a normal person. He has to spread himself out. He shakes Mum's hand without even leaning forward.

"Well…" he says.

He doesn't look impressed.

"AJ would do a little better in PE if he could show some enthusiasm. What do you think, AJ, any chance?"

I shrug.

Mum's staring at him.

"What do you mean?" she says.

"Well, if he could run around the track without giving up and lying down, that would be a start."

Mum looks confused.

"Is it a very big track?"

"It's just normal size, Mum," I mumble.

"But AJ loves running," she says. "He loves it!"

She's shouting now.

"He loves running! Don't you, AJ? Tell him!"

Mr. Higgins looks astonished. He puts both his feet on the floor, probably because he might fall off his chair otherwise. People are pretending not to look, which means they're all glancing at us, then looking away.

I'm so embarrassed. If I could just die now and be carried out on my chair and never have to see any of these people again, that would be fine. Or if the ceiling could fall in, everyone would have to be evacuated and no one would remember how it all started.

Mum nudges me.

"Sorry," she whispers.

Mr. Higgins raises his eyebrows.

"Well, problem solved then," he says. "I look forward to seeing you in action, AJ."

Then he stands up. Just to make sure we go.

I'm stuck to my seat. I think my legs might collapse under me and I won't be able to actually get out of the hall. Just to finish things off. Why couldn't he say something nice so we could leave the room with a bit of dignity? I hate him. What an idiot he is.

STARS

As we walk out of the school I can feel Mum getting smaller and smaller beside me. I know I should smile at her but I can't. It's been one of the most embarrassing experiences of my life (and there've been a few).

Mum doesn't speak until we're right out of the grounds.

"I put my foot in it, didn't I?" she says.

"You could have just shut up," I say. "We were nearly finished."

"You said I could speak."

"Yeah, well. Bad idea, wasn't it?"

"I'm sorry, AJ."

She looks even more upset than me. Because she almost never gets things right and at least I do sometimes.

"Forget it," I say. "I hate him anyway."

She puts her arm through mine.

"Can we go to the Olympic Park?" she says.

"Okay."

It's dark when we get there and the stadium looks fantastic all lit up. We walk a little way along the river and stand and look at the sky. It's orange and full of clouds but we can still see some stars.

"Don't you like running anymore?" Mum says.

"I don't know. I'm growing out of it I suppose."

Mum sighs.

"What you said to Aisha, is it true?" she says. "Are we all made of stardust?"

"Yes," I say.

"So you and me are made of the same stuff? And everyone else?"

"We all are."

She smiles.

"When I was little I used to come here with Grandad," she says. "I always wanted to touch a star but I couldn't reach. One night he said, 'If I put you on my shoulders you can take a star and put it in your pocket.' So I sat on his shoulders and took a star and put it in my pocket. And it's still there."

"What do you mean?"

"I've always got that star in my pocket. It doesn't matter what pocket I've got. It's always there."

We stand by the river for ages. I try to imagine the sky's completely clear and we can see shooting stars and the only sound is trees blowing in the breeze. But really there's the sound of sirens in the distance and people shouting and the stars don't budge, except after a while they disappear behind the clouds. But while we can see them they're beautiful.

FEET ARE FEET

I'm going to have to become someone else. I can't run anymore and I can't be funny like Harvey so I'm going to be the kid who hates sports. I'm walking to PE wearing a face that says *I hate running*.

Mr. Higgins is waiting for me outside the changing room.

"AJ," he says, "I've got a job for you."

"What?"

"If you don't want to do PE, you can make yourself useful. Come on."

I can't believe my luck. I have to stop myself from bouncing down the corridor behind him. I don't want to look too keen.

I've never been in the PE office before. There are piles of papers all over the table and sports magazines on the shelves and posters of athletes on the wall. And there's a trash bin overflowing with coffee cups and candy wrappers. They're spilling onto the floor.

Mr. Higgins pulls a box full of running shoes out from under the table.

"Right," he says, "sort these for me, will you? They've been cluttering up the office for too long. Match them up and put them in order of size."

There's loads of them. I can't believe how many there are.

"Got it?" he says.

I nod and he goes.

Some of the shoes look brand-new, like they came straight out of a box. How can someone leave a brand-new pair of shoes at school and not come back to find them? There are really old ones too with holes in the soles and bits of rubber hanging off like mine and there's a pair with hearts scribbled all over and initials.

You can tell a lot by what a shoe looks like. It must be like a forensic science. I expect you can tell which foot someone kicks a ball with or how they walk or where they've been just by looking at the sole.

Anyway, there are twelve pairs of shoes and two odd ones (both left foot) and I put them on the floor in order of size, from size three to size eleven. When I've finished I pick up a running magazine and read about what to eat before a race (porridge is good). I can hear kids doing PE outside but I don't mind. I like it here. I think maybe I should be a PE teacher when I grow up.

When Mr. Higgins comes back he looks pleased.

"Good job," he says. "Now, one of the perks of doing that, apart from seeing the inside of my office, is you get first pick. Take a pair for yourself."

I'm not sure what he means so I don't move. I don't want to embarrass myself.

"Go on," he says. "There must be something that fits."

I was size five in the summer but I must be six now. There's one pair that's six. They look brand-new except for a label inside that says ANIKA SHARMA.

"Try them on. Go on."

I put them on. They feel great. Mr. Higgins crouches down next to me and feels the end of the shoe.

"Can you wriggle your toes?"

I wriggle my toes.

"Okay," he says, "they're yours."

"They've got 'Anika Sharma' in them," I say.

(I don't know why I say this. I feel like I have to say something.)

His eyes flash.

"Feet are feet, lad."

"Who is she?"

"No idea. I don't think she spent a lot of time in PE, do you?"

I'm staring at my feet. I can't believe the shoes are going to be mine.

"Well?" he says.

"Can I keep them?"

"Yes. They've been here a year. No use to me."

I have to stop myself from running out of the office. I want to make sure he doesn't change his mind but I don't want to look desperate. I put my school shoes back on and put the running shoes in my bag. It takes about a hundred years.

"Thanks." I grunt.

Part of me wants to put them back on and run around the track. And part of me feels like maybe I can't run anymore except in socks on the stairs. Like maybe I've been kidding myself.

As soon as I'm home I peel the labels out of the shoes. I think about writing *AJ* inside but then I think, *What if Anika Sharma wants them back? That would be really embarrassing.* So I don't. I put them under my bed. I don't even try them on again. I feel a bit superstitious. I think they need to live here for a few days before I can think of them as mine. But I also feel really excited.

SPECIAL

When I first started school, my teacher told me my mum and dad were special. She said how lucky I was but she didn't say it like how lucky I'd be if Mum and Dad were Hollywood film stars. She said it sort of sympathetically. Like if I'd gotten a new kitten but it only had three legs.

I told Grandad when we were walking home from school and he said, "Well, they're special to me and they're special to you, but I'm not sure how they are special to your teacher. Has she ever met them?"

I told him she met Mum one time when we made pizza and parents came in to help. And I remember I thought Mum was excited but now I think she was probably nervous. But my teacher was really nice to her.

Then Grandad said, "What I think she meant is that your mum and dad are different, and sometimes people think being different is a problem but actually it can be a very nice thing. Not everyone likes other people who are different. But to me, they're just people."

He said it really carefully and then he said, "Do you understand?"

I sort of understood so I sort of nodded.

Then he lifted me onto his shoulders. I loved that. I just loved it. He was tall and so that made me the tallest person in the street. I couldn't see a single person who was taller than me. Not the lollipop lady and not the ice cream man in his van outside the school. Not even the window cleaner, because even though he had a ladder he was cleaning the ground-floor windows. It made me think if I could be anything I'd be a bird.

VICTOR

Aisha's dangling off the school gate.

"Can we go to the park?" she says.

"Okay."

I must be smiling.

"Are you in a good mood?" says Aisha. "Because you've been horrible lately."

"Yes," I say, "I'm in a good mood because I'm seeing you."

When we get to the park the girl with the Minnie Mouse ears is there, the one who probably won't be Aisha's friend. She's still wearing the ears. She's doing cartwheels in the play area and she's pretty good. Aisha's on the swing but she's not really enjoying it. Because this girl can do something I've never seen Aisha do. She does this funny backflip and then turns it into a cartwheel. Aisha's face! It's hilarious.

Aisha gets off the swing and does a little dance like she's on a high wire when in fact she's on that soft stuff that stops you from breaking your bones if you fall off the climbing bars. Then she does four cartwheels. If the fence hadn't gotten in her way I don't think she'd ever have stopped.

"That was good," I say.

She shrugs and walks away.

I follow her around the pond. Victor's sitting on the bench with his bag of bread, geese pecking around his feet.

Aisha stops in front of him.

"You know bread makes the geese ill?" she says.

(Did I tell you she's fearless?)

Victor looks surprised.

"Does it?"

"A vet came to our school and told us," Aisha says. "It makes their wings go bent. And then they can't fly. You think you're being nice to them but you're not really. Same with ducks."

Victor looks like his whole world's collapsed. He comes to the pond every day. It's his retired person's job.

"I used to feed them bread myself," says Aisha, "but now I know better."

Victor looks at the geese and then at Aisha.

"Bread's all I've got. I'm not going to give them sausages, am I?"

"I think they're vegetarian anyway," Aisha says.

Victor sighs.

"You know a lot about them, don't you? You're not a park-keeper, are you?"

"Maybe," says Aisha. "I might be."

She seems to be growing in height.

"Really?" says Victor.

"I'm not a park-keeper exactly," she says. "I'm a sort of park-keeper volunteer. I like to keep an eye on the ducks because they're my favorites. And the geese."

It's awkward.

"What can I feed them?" he says.

"Frozen peas are good," says Aisha, "when they're not frozen anymore. Or bits of peel, like if you peel potatoes or something."

Victor nods.

"Can I give the bread to the squirrels?" he says.

"I don't know," says Aisha. "I only know about geese and ducks."

We leave Victor sitting on the bench with his bag of bread.

"Well, that was embarrassing, Aisha," I say.

She shrugs.

"I had to tell him."

"Did you?"

She nods.

"Yes," she says. "People have to have information. Then they can make decisions."

"Right," I say.

I look back at Victor. He's watching us go.

"I bet as soon as we're gone he'll give them the bread," I say.

"I bet he won't," says Aisha.

NUMBER GRIDS

I'm trying not to watch Josephine as she collapses onto a kitchen chair. She's literally moving in slow motion. She looks like she might end up on the floor.

"I've just got to sit quietly for a moment," she says.

Except Josephine can't sit quietly.

We watch the tea brew. Mum's scrubbed out the glass jug and the tea bags are floating on top of the water. I suppose they must do that in teapots too, it's just that you can't see them.

"I'll buy you a new teapot, Alice," says Josephine.

"You will not buy me a new teapot," says Mum.

"Why not?"

"I like the jug."

Aisha looks up from her work. She's actually got homework today. She's drawing a number grid.

"Why do you like the jug, Alice?" she says.

"Because it's mine," says Mum.

Josephine sighs.

"What's your homework, Aisha?" she says. "What are you trying to do?"

"Well," says Aisha, "I've got twelve sweets to share between four children. I have to work out how many they get each. I'm drawing a number grid."

"I don't think you need a number grid," Josephine says. "Not to divide four into twelve. Don't they teach you times tables?"

She starts to recite the four times table really slowly, like Aisha's stupid.

Aisha puts her hands over her ears.

"I'm doing it the way the teacher says."

Josephine rolls her eyes.

"Okay. Sorry. Can I show you after then?"

Aisha nods.

It takes Aisha ages to do her number grid and all the time Josephine's drumming her fingers on the table.

"Do you have to do number grids, AJ?" Josephine says. "At secondary school."

I shrug. I don't want to get involved.

"Three," says Aisha angrily. "They get three sweets each."

"Well done, yes," says Josephine. "But you can't

draw a grid every time you need to know how many times four goes into twelve."

Then she recites the four times table again. Only this time she writes it down as she says it.

"That means four children times three sweets makes twelve sweets altogether. Simple."

Aisha shrugs.

"Don't shrug, sweetheart, just because AJ does it. You're not a teenager yet," Josephine says.

Mum gets up, fills the kettle, and walks into the garden. It's cold out there but she's not coming in.

The kettle's boiling. I ignore it (which isn't easy, I can tell you). Josephine gets up and switches it off at the plug. I look at her through the cloud of steam. She looks hot and annoyed and really, really pregnant, like if she's not careful she'll have the baby right there and then in the kitchen.

FORCE FIELD

I'm walking across the school field when I see Amit on the track. He's mostly jogging but every now and then he does a little sprint. And he's fast. I don't watch for too long—in fact, I try to look as though I'm not watching at all—but one thought fills my head: I've got to start training properly.

When I get home I put on the running shoes. They feel great. I jog on the spot in my room for a bit and then I run down to the front door. But when

I get there it's like there's a force field pushing me back. I turn around. Dad's watching me.

"What's wrong?" he says.

"I was going for a run," I say, "but I can't."

"Because Grandad won't be there?" he says.

I nod.

Dad looks at the floor.

"What I think," he says, "is when something good happens it never goes away."

"What do you mean?"

"I think Grandad's still running with you in the park. And I think he's in the garden with me."

It's the longest thing Dad's said to me for ages.

"So you won't be on your own," he says. "He'll be there."

"Do you think so?"

He looks a bit embarrassed.

"Yes," he says.

And the force field between me and the door comes down.

ALL THE FOOTSTEPS

I run out onto the pavement. It's weird running in new shoes. I jog past Grandad's house, not looking at it, and race to the park. I forget even to look in the convenience store. I'm lost in the sound of my feet on the ground.

The park's empty apart from Victor on his bench

and a small boy being pushed on the swings by his mum.

It's a bit of a shock to be running to be honest. It takes me a while to find a rhythm. I don't exactly see Grandad but I can sort of feel him beside me so I don't feel alone. Like all the footsteps we took together are coming with me too.

I look up into the sky and listen to my breath and the sound of my heart beating. It's beginning to rain. Small drops are landing on my face. They feel so nice. It's like I've had a big injection of happiness. My whole body's buzzing.

Victor waves as I run past. There's potato peel and soggy peas scattered around his bench. Ducks and geese are pecking around his feet. I have to swerve so I don't slip. It looks like a fox ripped open a garbage bag.

GET A CAFÉ

If I'm on top of the world, Mum's the opposite. If there was a big hole, she'd be sitting in it.

"AJ," she says, "you've been running."

She's trying to smile but she looks so sad.

"How was your day, Mum?"

"Well," she says, "I got the biscuits muddled up. It took ages to sort out."

I make some tea and we sit at the table. I feel even worse about the teapot now. She could really do with something nice to look at. The cloud's right above her head and it's making a really big shadow.

"What job would you do if you could do anything?" I say.

(I'm in an anything-is-possible mood.)

"I'd be an air hostess flying around from one place to the next. Except I wouldn't want to leave you. I'd have to be back in time for tea."

She smiles.

"I couldn't do that, could I?"

I shake my head.

"Why don't you make cakes and sell them?" I say. "If you made one really big cake and it cost five pounds to make and you cut it into ten slices, you could sell each slice for two pounds and you'd make...*ding ding ding ding*...fifteen pounds...lots of money. And that's just for one cake."

Mum looks interested.

"Where would I sell it?" she says.

"Get a café," I say, "where there's lots of old people and kids. Old people love eating cakes in cafés. Some of them do it all day. And kids too."

"You can't just get a café!" says Mum. "You have to have plates and cups and tables and chairs."

"People could bring their own cups and plates."

"Who'd wash them?"

"They could take them home to wash," I say. "It would make it special."

"Get people to bring their own cups and plates to the café? AJ! People wouldn't come."

"Wouldn't they?"

"People go to cafés so they don't have to wash up!"

She's shouting.

"Well, why don't you sell your cakes in the park café? It's open again."

Mum's shaking her head.

"I couldn't go back. I couldn't, AJ. I'd be too embarrassed."

"But you used to work there and they liked you. And you make the best cakes ever."

"No, AJ!" she shouts. "I can't do it! I can't."

PLASTIC FLOWERS

Sometimes when I'm running I think I'm making the world turn and if I stop the world might stop turning too. I know it's stupid but that's what I think. I'm running around our little park in my new shoes and I'm about to meet Crystal so what I do is I run slower and slower until I'm walking. That way if the world stops everything might not just fly off. And the world doesn't stop. In fact, nothing changes at all except I get my breath back. I suppose someone started running somewhere else.

Crystal's waiting outside the café. With Harvey.

"Look who I bumped into," she says.

"So what are you two doing?" says Harvey.

"Getting chips," says Crystal.

"Can I come?" Harvey says. "I've got some money."

It's up to Crystal. I don't have money so I can't really say.

"Come on then," says Crystal.

We're stuck at the back of the line for ages while families order about five million different drinks and little kids keep changing their minds. It's fancier than when Mum used to work here. There's a children's corner with books and toys and there are new shelves with biscuits, chips, and slices of cake in cellophane wrappers but they don't have any whole cakes like Mum's. I wish she'd bring hers but, in case you haven't noticed, one thing about my mum is if she doesn't want to do something she won't. There's no point even arguing.

When we get to the counter I see the woman with hoop earrings who used to run things before it was all done up. I stare out the window as if there's something really interesting going on outside, like a squirrel being chased up a tree. I've got this feeling that if she sees me she'll say something embarrassing.

We sit outside and eat our chips. There's a pot of plastic flowers on the table. Someone's taken one out and stuck it in the ketchup bottle.

"Did you hear about the boy who stole flowers from a graveyard for Mother's Day?" says Harvey. "He gave them to his mum and that night there was a storm and everything blew out of the house except for the flowers."

"Really?" I say. "Really? Wow, that's amazing."

"It's true," he says. "I saw it on the Internet."

"Yeah," I say, "and I saw on the Internet that your brain's the size of a peanut."

Someone else might be offended but he's not bothered. He takes the flower out of the bottle and squeezes ketchup all over the chips.

Crystal pulls a bit of paper out of her pocket.

"Do you want to see my drawing?" she says.

She opens it on the table. It's a round symmetrical pattern with little drawings in it of Bunsen burners and test tubes and a sun and moon in the middle and all the letters of the alphabet around the outside.

"What is it?" says Harvey.

"It's like a mandala," she says. "It's a symbol of peace. It goes on forever. That's why it's round."

"Can you make me one?" says Harvey.

"No," she says, "make your own."

We eat our chips and watch the little kids trip over or fall off their scooters. It's cold and they're all wrapped up in padded coats so it doesn't hurt but they still cry. I never really noticed before how much little kids cry. There's never one moment when they're all completely happy.

Then we hang around the park for a couple of hours, not really doing anything, just talking. We even sit with Victor for a bit and talk about the meaning of life. (He doesn't think there is one so it doesn't take long.) He's eating a tuna-and-peanut-butter sandwich. It smells revolting.

And Harvey kicks things. For someone who

doesn't like football he spends a lot of time kicking things.

WRONG FEET

It's the school cross-country trials and I've got all these terrifying thoughts going around my head—me falling over, me missing the race, Anika Sharma wanting her shoes back. And when I've run out of things to worry about I go right back to the beginning and worry about them all over again. It's like being stuck on a roundabout and feeling sicker and sicker but not being able to get off.

It's tutor period and I'm wondering what would happen if I put my shoes on the wrong feet when Miss Charmant says my name.

"And AJ for making a good effort in French," she says.

What?

Crystal leans across to me.

"You're getting a prize for French."

"AJ handed all his homework in on time and worked hard on his vocabulary," says Miss Charmant. "Well done, AJ."

Then she reads out some more names. Crystal's getting prizes for Math and Biology. Harvey's getting a prize for Creative Writing. I can imagine that. He's always making things up. He probably writes brilliant stories.

"And what that means," says Miss Charmant when she's finished, "is you are invited to a special evening where you will collect your certificates in front of parents and guardians. Well done, all of you."

I don't know if anyone else is excited but I'm not. Mum and Dad will hate it. Harvey looks pretty pleased though.

SCHOOL CROSS-COUNTRY TRIALS

About forty boys walk onto the field. I'm one of them. I'm hoping it'll be okay because I watched the girls' trials yesterday and the girl with the strongest finish came first. And I've got a strong finish.

Groups of kids are standing around the field watching or just hanging out eating their packed lunches. Crystal and Harvey wave.

"Right," says Mr. Higgins as we huddle at the starting line. "No pushing, shoving, tripping, or stopping. Three times around the field. Go!"

We thin out really quickly. Amit goes straight to the front and I'm not far behind, just keeping pace. After the first lap I keep level with him and on the second lap I overtake him. He's having to run really fast to keep up because I'm flying.

But as I approach the finish line all my strength ebbs away. I keep going but I can't do my usual sprint and Amit pushes ahead. He beats me by about two strides. I'm not kidding! I'm that close. And he's been training for weeks. So even though I didn't win I feel pleased with myself.

Mr. Higgins comes over.

"So," he says, "your mum was right."

He high-fives me.

"You're through to the interschool tournament."

I can't speak so I don't. I imagine his testosterone running down my arm and wonder if it will make me stronger but I don't feel anything except slightly awkward. Amit comes over.

"You should train on the track sometime," he says.

I wonder if he's smirking but he doesn't seem to be.

"Okay," I say.

I'm trying to stop myself from looking too enthusiastic.

I walk over to Crystal and Harvey.

"Well done," Crystal says. "That was fast."

Harvey's looking at me like I'm a different person. His mouth's actually hanging open. He's got a bit of gum in it.

"Could you always run like that?" he says.

I nod. "My shoes didn't fit."

He looks at my feet.

"You got new ones?"

"Yeah."

He smiles.

"I wonder if that would work for me," he says.

Then he turns and walks away and as he crosses the field he spits his gum onto the grass.

BIRTHDAY PRESENT

"I hope you like your birthday present," Aisha says. "I chose it myself."

"I'm sure I will," I say.

"I got it on the weekend," she says.

She's playing invisible hopscotch on the pavement, doing these funny little jumps.

"And Mum and Dad are getting you two presents."

"Sounds good," I say.

"They're to do with running but don't ask me anything else," she says.

"I haven't asked you anything yet."

"Well, don't," she says. "It's a secret."

I don't need to ask. They must be getting me running shoes. Grandad got them for me last year. If Mum and Dad get me them too, I could end up with three pairs. It would be embarrassing but I'd cope.

DROP-DEAD GORGEOUS

I've got to ask Josephine about Tyler. She's having a cup of tea and she doesn't stay often. I need her to tell me about Tyler because I need to persuade him to let me see the Olympic track now that I'm running again. I need to know if he likes a particular chocolate or if he's got a favorite song or something. I want to know if he's got a heart because if he has I want to find a way into it (especially after the coffee-in-the-car incident).

"How did you meet Tyler?" I say.

I say it really quietly so she can pretend she didn't hear.

"She met him at a fair," says Aisha.

She's drawing turrets on a castle.

"She was on the bumper cars and she saw him and she fell in love"—she puts up her hands and wiggles her fingers—"and she wanted to marry him."

"Not quite," says Josephine, "but yes, I met him at a fair."

"And then she wanted to marry him," says Aisha.

"I did, I thought that's the man for me."

"Why?" I say.

"Well," she says, "he was just..."

She looks into the distance. Not right into the distance so she's looking at the garden but into the middle distance where no one can catch her eye.

"Drop-dead gorgeous," she says.

Ugh. Did she really say that? That is so embarrassing.

"Mum!" Aisha screams.

I wish I'd never asked. I hope she hasn't mixed Tyler up with someone else.

Then Aisha writes down *drop dead gorguss* and

draws a little stick man and an arrow pointing to the words.

"Did he make you want to drop down dead?" she says.

Josephine sort of smiles. She looks really tired, like she might be just about to drop down dead now.

"It was a little while ago," she says.

"Would you still say he's gorgeous?" I say.

"Yes, AJ, he's lovely."

Grandad would say I'm pushing it now but the words are falling out.

"He just doesn't seem very lovely to me," I say.

"Because he won't take you to the stadium?" says Josephine. She's looking quite annoyed.

"Maybe."

"Well, if you don't mind me saying, AJ," she says, "you're not very lovely yourself."

"It's because he's a teenager," says Aisha. "That's why he broke the teapot by deliberate. Only teenagers do that. And toddlers."

I might have known. Why is it that every conversation criticizing someone else ends up criticizing me? Is everyone else perfect?

USAIN BOLT'S AUTOGRAPH

I'm training with Amit after school. It's weird because I always thought he was my enemy but actually he's okay. He just can't help being annoying. It's like we'll be talking and suddenly he'll drop down and do some jumping jacks or push-ups and I'm left talking to myself. And he doesn't even realize it's annoying.

And the other thing I've realized about Amit is he's still good-looking, even up close. He hasn't hit the ugly-teen stage early like me. He'll probably be one of those kids who pass right through their teens without a single pimple. Not that I care. No one notices the kid who comes second.

But the weirdest thing is that sometimes Mr.

Higgins comes out and gives us advice. Today he says, "You're a bit heavy on your feet, AJ. Think gazelle, not elephant."

And so I'm running around the track trying to think of myself as a gazelle and you know what, it works for about three minutes.

But the very best thing about being on the track is I'm exactly where I should be. And sometimes the primary school kids next door peer through the fence and watch. I'm not kidding! I have to stop myself from smiling. I don't want to look like an idiot.

Anyway, now that I'm sort of friends with Amit I have to ask him about Usain Bolt. So as we walk out of school I say, "What was it like seeing Usain Bolt right up close?"

"It was amazing," he says.

His eyes are shining.

"It was the best moment of my life. Do you want to see the autograph?"

"Yeah, will you bring it in?"

"I've got it here," he says.

"What?"

My heart feels like it's going to break out of my chest. I'm not kidding you. I have to take a few slow, deep breaths.

Amit's beaming. He rummages through his bag and from right at the bottom pulls out a scrunched-up ticket and hands it to me. It's a bit of a shock to be honest. It looks as though it's been through a washing machine. I can still just about see Usain Bolt's autograph but the ink's faded and smudged.

"What happened to it?" I say.

"I left it in my pocket," he says. "Mum washed it."

I can't speak. The thing I wanted most in the world has gone down the drain. Literally. It's probably come out of somebody's tap by now and been used to boil potatoes.

"My mum was going to put it in a frame," he says, "but I wouldn't let her. I carried it around in my pocket for ages. Like forever."

He looks a bit embarrassed.

"I was only seven," he says.

I hold the ticket for a few moments and then give it back to him. I'm worried it might fall apart in my hand.

"Why do you carry it around?"

He shrugs.

"It's lucky."

"It's going to fall apart," I say.

"I know," he says.

He puts it back in his bag.

I can't help feeling sorry for Amit. I know he's not the sort of person you should feel sorry for but I can't help it. He's got the most precious thing in the world and it looks rubbish.

When I get home I take the newspaper cutting of Grandad at the Canada Cup final out of its frame and I take my Olympic ticket out of the collage and I swap them. (Grandad looks great next to Usain Bolt by the way.) Then I put the collage back on the wall and the framed ticket under my bed. I've got a plan but I need to think about it for a while in case I change my mind.

GRANDAD'S HOUSE

We hear the men taking down the scaffolding before we see them. They're yelling and telling jokes and throwing the metal poles onto the back of a truck. And in front of Grandad's house there's a FOR SALE sign.

"Look, AJ!" Aisha screams. "It's for sale! Mum and Dad can buy it and we can be neighbors."

She bounces down the pavement like she's got springs on her feet. When I catch up she's standing on our doorstep.

"You know," she says, "your door's quite scruffy. Why don't you paint it?"

It's red but the paint's chipping off. It is pretty scruffy.

"Not good enough for you, is it?" I say, and she laughs.

"Just saying."

Aisha's so excited she can't stop jumping around. (I have to admit it would be pretty amazing to have her as a neighbor.) She crashes into the garden to see Dad and she chokes on her toast because she can't sit still. And then she gets hiccups.

When Mum arrives home Aisha's trying to drink a glass of water upside down for the third time.

"What's the world record for hiccups?" says Aisha.

"I don't know—ten years?" I say. "Maybe even fifty."

Aisha's chin's wobbling.

"Get her some toffees, AJ," Mum says, and pulls some change out of her bag.

Aisha thinks toffees cure her hiccups. She says the chewing helps. It's a bit suspicious if you ask me. I don't mind, though. I get to go to the convenience store.

I run to the store. A man's standing on a step-ladder loading cans of dog food onto a shelf. The amazing girl's behind the counter looking at her phone. The candies are laid out next to the till but I'm having trouble concentrating. When I find the toffees I hold out the packet.

The girl puts down her phone.

"Anything else?" she says.

I want to say, *Will you marry me?* (In a sort of cool way, if that's possible.) *Not now of course*, I'd say, *when I'm older. I know I'm only eleven and I look pretty ugly but I might be more appealing when I'm a French-speaking international athlete.*

She's waiting for an answer.

"No thanks," I say.

She smiles. Did I tell you she's got amazing eyes? They're not like Aisha's at all. Aisha's eyes are full of light; this girl's eyes are full of mystery.

"Fifty pence," she says.

I give her the money. As I put it in her hand her phone pings.

"Thanks," she says.

Then she's picking up her phone.

Aisha and Mum are making up a recipe for peanut-butter-and-orange biscuits when I get back. Aisha's stopped hiccupping. She eats the toffees anyway.

When Josephine arrives Aisha says, "Can we buy Grandad's house?"

Josephine shakes her head.

"No, Aisha, sorry."

"But you grew up there," she says.

"Yes, but it belonged to the factory," says Josephine. "And we can't afford it."

Aisha's eyes fill with tears.

"I'm sorry, love," says Josephine, "but we're not where the money is."

It makes me worry about Mum and Dad, because they're even less where the money is.

LUCKY

Miss Charmant is saying nice things about everyone. It's the last tutor period before half term and she wants us all to feel good. She's the nicest teacher in the world. If I ever become a teacher (and I might if I can't be an athlete), I want to be like Miss Charmant.

The other teachers are in a pretty good mood too; they all can't wait for a week off either. When the bell goes everyone races out of the school except me and Amit. We're having one last run on the track.

We're just warming up when Mr. Higgins appears.

"Good lads," he says. "Remember, STRIVE—strength, tenacity, rigor, impetus, values, energy."

Amit mumbles the words with him but I just stare at my feet. I don't really like that sort of thing. It's awkward. Then he high-fives us and he's gone.

We're walking out of the grounds together when I get my framed Olympic ticket out of my bag. I've gotten used to it not being on my wall. I hold it out to Amit.

"Do you want this?" I say.

I feel a bit embarrassed so I sort of mutter. Amit stares at the ticket. He doesn't know what I mean.

"I thought you might want one that hasn't been through the washing machine," I say. "You can put your autographed ticket in the frame too. And you can put it on your wall."

He takes it from me and just stares at it. His mouth's fallen open.

"Are you sure?"

"Yes."

He can't quite believe it.

"The frame too?" he says.

I nod. I want to be sure it doesn't end up in the wash.

"Don't you want it?"

"I've got my grandad's ticket."

He gets his autographed ticket out from the bottom of his bag and holds it against the frame.

He's smiling so much his face sort of explodes.

"Thank you!" he says. "Thank you, thank you."

He puts the tickets in his bag and hurries across the field, like he can't get home quick enough. Then he stops, looks back at me, and does the Lightning Bolt. It's an embarrassing moment. He's better-looking than me and cleverer than me but he's also really uncool.

When I get home I realize I've done myself a favor too because my Olympic ticket will be touching Usain Bolt's signature. And that's got to be lucky.

HALF TERM

This half term's going to be rubbish because Grandad's not here. He used to take me and Aisha out at half term. We'd collect conkers in the park and have picnics or go to the museums. I don't want to spend the whole week missing him so I'm going to run as much as I can. Because running gets rid of my worries. It's like shaking the dust out of a blanket—all these little bits fall out and then you can smooth it flat. It sends a magic chemical to your brain to cheer you up. It just zaps in. I don't think you could stop it, even if you wanted to.

I'm meeting Crystal and Harvey in the climbing area at the Olympic Park. I jog the whole way there.

It's packed with little kids but we hang around for ages climbing the ropes. Then we walk along the river, sit on a bench, and eat chips.

"Did you hear about the boy who swallowed a magnet?" Harvey says.

"Tell us," I say. "I can't wait."

"He always faces north now," says Harvey. "He can't help it. It's the only way he feels comfortable."

"That's rubbish," says Crystal. "That's the most stupid thing you've ever said."

"It's true," says Harvey. "It was on the Internet."

It's cloudy and cold but we sit for ages trying to make up stories more ridiculous than Harvey's. Suddenly there's a crack of lightning. The geese rise up in a flurry and rain crashes down. It's drumming on the path and making little points on top of the water. People put up umbrellas or pull on raincoats. We run to a tree and stand under it. Crystal's got her jacket over her head. She's shivering.

"Do you want to come over and watch a film?" Harvey says. "You can stay for tea."

I shake my head. I want to go to the little park. I don't even know why.

"I'll stay out," I say.

"Are you sure, AJ?" says Crystal.

She looks apologetic. Water's dripping off her nose.

"Really," I say. "You two go."

ELECTRIC BLANKET

The little park's completely empty. Even Victor's not here. I feel like a ghost. The path's wet and shiny and the red dots look like they're jumping off the ground.

I run around the path as fast as I can. I've got this feeling it would be really bad luck if I stop so I run through the rain until I'm soaked and exhausted. I might have just run my fastest time ever.

As I arrive at the gate the rain stops and a rainbow appears over the park. A woman and a little boy are walking in. The boy's carrying a bag of conkers. He looks up at the rainbow and points. And suddenly I have this awful feeling. I think it might pass but it doesn't. It stays right with me. I do a slow jog the whole way home, really concentrating on the sound of my feet on the pavement so I don't have to think about how bad I feel.

Mum's sitting at the table when I get in. She's peeling potatoes.

"AJ," she says, "you're soaked."

"I'm all right," I say, and sit down next to her.

She puts her arm around my shoulder.

"What's wrong?"

It takes me a while to work out what's wrong and when I do I tell her.

"I thought if I ran around the park in my fastest time ever Grandad would come back. And I ran really fast and I thought he'd be waiting at the gate but he wasn't."

It sounds ridiculous when I say it out loud but Mum doesn't think it's ridiculous at all.

"When your nan died," she says, "I stood on a stool all afternoon to make her come back. And she didn't come back," she says. "And Grandad won't come back either."

She taps her chest.

"But they're in here, AJ," she says. "Both of them."

One thing Grandad left when he died was his electric blanket. It's pink and bobbly and it smells of his house. Sometimes if it was cold he would put it over me and Aisha while we watched TV. We got to keep it after he died because Josephine said she didn't want that nasty thing in her house. It's okay though because Aisha sometimes wraps herself up in it here. And that's what I do now. I wrap myself up in the blanket and I sit really still and I feel like I never, ever, ever want to move.

EVERYONE

Me and Crystal had a conversation once and it kind of changed the way I think. Crystal said, "Would you want another life after this one if you couldn't choose who you come back as?"

So you couldn't choose to come back as the rich

kids who live in the fancy new flats or the kid whose dad is a footballer. You could be born a boy or a girl and you could come back anywhere in the world. You could be born really poor or in a war or somewhere you can't go to school or as a kid who has to find things to sell from a rubbish pile.

In the end Crystal said she'd take the chance and I said I wouldn't, which was pretty depressing actually. Anyway, we talked about it for ages and then we had a horrible thought. Maybe we do have to come back over and over, as everyone, and if we do we'd better treat everyone well or we'll regret it when we have to be them. So when I walk past anyone in the street begging I feel really bad if I can't give them something (which is usually) or if I see someone taking something into Easy Exchange I feel terrible because that could be me.

THE SEA

Me, Mum, Dad, and Aisha are going to Southend for the day. We're going to have a picnic on the beach. Dad's nervous but he wants to come because he loves the sea. Mum's made sandwiches and cake and Dad's put soup in a thermos and we've got sun hats and raincoats and umbrellas and blankets because the forecast said sun and rain. Mum's got buckets and spades and Aisha's brought (can you believe it?) her hula hoop.

Tyler takes us to the station. His car still smells of old damp coffee. It's revolting. Everyone's wincing except me. I'm trying to pretend it smells of roses.

"Have fun," Tyler says when he drops us off. "And try not to be an idiot, AJ."

"You can count on me," I say.

We pile into the train and squeeze around a table. Dad looks worried.

"What do you want to do when we get there, Eddie?" says Aisha.

"Sleep on the beach," he says.

"I'm going to make a castle," says Aisha.

"You're going to play with your hula hoop," I say, "seeing as we're taking it all that way."

"Of course," she says.

When we get to the beach we grab a patch of sand and lay out all our stuff. The sea looks like a massive whale stretched out in the distance. Families are putting up umbrellas and deck chairs and kids are kicking balls around. Aisha sees a couple of teenagers lying on the sand wrapped up in a coat.

"What are they doing?" she says.

"Keeping warm," I say.

"That's disgusting," she says.

She picks up her hula hoop and moves along the beach and we pick up our stuff and follow.

"That's better."

Then she's hula-hooping. First she spins the hula hoop around her about a million times and then she takes a bow. Then she skips with it about a million times and takes a bow.

"Look, Alice!" she shouts.

Mum claps.

"Can you do that, AJ?"

"Yes, Mum, but I'm not going to."

We don't want to walk the hundred miles to the sea so we make a sand castle and dig a moat around it and Aisha runs down to fill her bucket. It takes her about an hour to get there and back. I'm not kidding.

Then we have our picnic. It's cold so we're eating the sandwiches under fleeces and blankets. When it starts to rain we put on our raincoats. It's not heavy rain. It's just a shower.

Dad lies down under a blanket and closes his eyes and we watch the rain dribble down his nose. He won't give up. He's determined to fall asleep on the beach. There are big clouds overhead and the sea's gone dark gray.

"See," I say to Aisha, "I told you water isn't blue."

She screws up her nose.

"Here," says Mum, "have an umbrella."

I can't remember when I last felt this happy. We're shivering on a beach and cold water's dripping down my back and the sandwiches are soggy and the sea's so far away it's going to take all afternoon to go for a paddle. But you know what? It's the best day ever.

FISHING

I'm going to where we scattered Grandad's ashes. Don't ask me why. I just want to. Does there have to be a reason for everything?

The sun's out and the sky's almost completely blue and I'm running along the river path. It's cold but it's perfect for running. I dodge past people and dogs and cyclists and little kids pointing at things. Sometimes someone grabs their little kid in case I mow them down but I never would. Never. I'd throw myself into the river rather than knock over a little kid. That's what I'm like.

When I get to the bench I sit down and think about Grandad. He didn't want a grave. He talked about it, even though he didn't know he was going to die. He didn't want people to leave flowers and all that. He said he wouldn't be there anyway. And when he said that I thought about how bodies decompose into the earth and then I thought actually the whole world's like a massive recycling plant where everything gets used again and again. I thought I was pretty clever. I told Grandad and he said, *Could be. Could be.* Because we used to talk about that sort of interesting thing. Grandad said you never really know all the answers, you just end up realizing you never will.

After about two minutes I'm cold so I get up and run again. There are fewer people the farther I go.

And then I see Tyler. He's fishing. He's wearing a hat with bits that go over his ears and he's sitting on a sort of film director's chair and he's got a thermos by his feet. I want to turn back but I can't because he's seen me. When I get to him I stop.

"Good to see you running," he says.

We stare at each other awkwardly.

"Have you caught any fish?"

He shakes his head.

"I don't really come here for the fish," he says. "It's the peace I like."

Of course he doesn't come for the fish. He just wants to get away from other human beings. I'm about to run on when the words I've been thinking since Grandad died pretty much fall out of my mouth.

"Why didn't you let me and Grandad on the Olympic track?" I say.

He puts down his fishing rod.

"You could have done and now it's too late."

"AJ," he says. "That was your dream, not your grandad's. Get a grip, will you?"

"But you don't understand," I say. "And now we can't ever do it."

Tyler sighs.

"You know," he says, "when I was a kid I hid in the toilets at the Oval all night. Just so I could see the West Indies play the next day."

"You didn't."

"I did. My parents thought I was at a friend's that night. I got a beating when they found out."

"Did you see the match?"

"Yes—best cricket I ever saw."

I can't believe it. He's just transformed from horrible, boring Tyler into the most amazing kid ever.

"That's so cool," I say.

He sort of smiles.

"You couldn't do that now," he says. "Too many sensors. But I do understand. Thing is, I've got a family now and if I let you go on the track I'd probably lose my job. And now would not be a good time to lose my job."

I should tell him it doesn't matter, not to worry, but I don't. I have to leave a little flicker of hope, just in case.

"Do you miss Grandad?" I say.

He looks out at the river. It's dappled with sunlight.

"Yup," he says. "He used to sit with me sometimes."

"Here?"

He smiles. A heron swoops down and dips its beak into the water. It doesn't come up with a fish.

"You're a lot like him, you know," he says. "If you'd just calm down and stop being a pain in the neck."

I think about what he said for a moment and decide to take it as a compliment.

"In what way am I like him?" I say.

"Well," he says, "you're funny. Sometimes. You're kind. And you're amazing with your mum and dad and Aisha. And of course you can run."

I can feel myself getting hot.

"Okay," I say, "got to go."

And I run off along the path and all the time I'm trying to imagine a boy sitting on a toilet in a cricket ground all night and that boy being Tyler. It's almost impossible to believe. It's like I've gone through a magic door and come out in another world.

I run until I reach another bridge and then I cross it and run back along the other side of the river. I forget even to look for Tyler. My head's full of the sound of my feet hitting the path and the rustling reeds and the geese on the dappled water.

TEAPOTS

I'm nearly home when a man comes out of his house and puts a box of stuff on his walk. I always look in people's boxes. One time I found an old light saber and I really wanted to take it. I was going to pretend it was for Aisha, but in the end I just couldn't. I knew it would be written all over my face that I wanted it for myself.

The box is full of old kitchen stuff—nasty egg-cups (one's got a bit of dried yolk on it) and some saucepans. And underneath there's a teapot. I don't want to break another teapot. That would probably be like a million years' bad luck. So I take all the other stuff out and line the eggcups on the wall. It's sort of embarrassing. I look like I'm admiring them when they're the ugliest eggcups you could ever see. They'd put you off the egg.

Then I lift the teapot out. It's really nice. It's got pink and gold flowers on the lid and around the pot and it looks very fragile. As I'm holding it the man comes out again with a pile of books. He rolls his eyes.

"Having a clear-out," he says.

"Don't you want this?" I say.

He shakes his head. "Do you like it?"

"My mum would."

He smiles.

"One minute."

He goes back inside and comes out carrying two little cups and saucers that match the pot.

"We've got two left if you'd like them."

"Don't you want them?"

He shakes his head.

"Nope," he says. "Please take them. My wife collects teapots. We have far too many."

I'm trying to think why someone would have more than one teapot but it seems rude to ask.

"Put them in the box if you like," he says.

He takes some newspaper out of his recycling bin and helps me wrap them. It's sort of awkward.

"If you're giving these away, the others must be amazing," I say.

He smiles.

"You know what," he says, "to me a teapot is just a teapot. It's the tea that counts."

He's speaking really quietly. It makes me wonder if his wife's inside making tea in one of her millions of teapots and doesn't know he's throwing this one out.

"But I hope your mum enjoys it."

I want to run home but I don't because I'm scared I'll smash the teapot and get a lifetime's bad luck so I do a weird fast walk, keeping a bit of one foot on the ground at all times, like an Olympic speed walker. I've also got to get away quickly in case his wife comes out and wants her teapot back.

When I get in I put the kettle on and wash the teapot and cups and saucers in case there's any egg yolk on them. Then I put them on the table with a mug for me. When I hear Mum come in I fill the pot.

"I've made tea," I shout.

"Okay," she says.

When she sees the table her face sort of melts.

"Where did you get them?" she says.

"I found them around the corner. Someone was throwing them out."

"Throwing them out! They're beautiful," she says.

Dad comes in and they're both standing there looking at the teapot and the cups and saucers.

"I'm sorry about the other teapot," I say.

"Never mention it again," Mum says. "This one's even nicer."

When Mum pours the tea, little drips run down the spout but she doesn't care. She reaches out and takes Dad's hand and mine.

"Aren't I lucky?" she says.

HALLOWEEN

Little kids are coming out of the primary school carrying pumpkins. As soon as we're home Aisha runs into the bathroom and comes out wearing a witch's costume. She stands in front of me proudly. She's painted her face green.

"Who are you and what have you done with my cousin?" I say.

"It's me, it's me!" she says.

She's screaming with laughter. It works every time.

She runs into the garden and I hear Dad say, "Who's this?" and she's screaming again. She's the funniest kid in the world. I'm not kidding.

Dad's carved a face into one of his pumpkins. He

puts it on the wall with a candle inside and lights it. It looks like it's winking.

I have to walk around the streets behind Aisha and hide behind hedges while she knocks on people's doors. Josephine and Tyler are working and Mum and Dad never go out at Halloween. In fact, they turn all the lights off so no one rings the doorbell.

"Aren't you getting dressed up?" Aisha says.

"No."

"Why not?"

"I'm Year 7."

"You can't walk with me then," she says.

"Don't worry, I'll hide," I say. "I just want to make sure no one eats you up or anything."

"It's a difficult age, isn't it?" she says. "You're too old to dress up but I expect you still want candy."

"Yes, I do," I say.

We wait until it's dark and then we set off. There's loads of little kids running up and down the streets. Aisha sees some friends and suddenly she's surrounded by witches and wizards. I keep as far behind her as I can, just close enough so I can see where she is. At one house I hear her say, "Can I have two please? One's for my little cousin—he's too afraid to come to the door." It's a bit embarrassing to be honest.

After about half an hour Aisha wants to go home. On the way back we pass a house with huge cobwebs draped across the door.

"I'll just try this one," she says.

She stands on the steps while I wait on the sidewalk. A boy opens the door, sees me, and screams.

"Argh! What's that? It's the scariest thing I've ever seen!"

It's Harvey.

"That's my cousin," says Aisha. "He always looks like that."

When we get home Aisha tips her candy onto the table and divides it into two piles.

"By the way," she says, "did you finish the chocolate shoe?"

"No, I hid it from you," I say.

"Right," she says. "I'll have some back then."

And she picks out a load of toffees and puts them in her pile. I don't mind though. I don't like toffee. I always think it's going to pull my teeth out.

INTERSCHOOL TOURNAMENT

The hockey team's using the minibus so Amit's mum is taking me to the interschool tournament. I've been ready for two hours and I'm trying not to get too excited. I found some porridge in the cupboard and cooked it up for slow-release energy like it said in the sports magazine. It was a bit lumpy to be honest. You can't get rid of lumps in porridge like you can with pancake batter.

I'm going to run straight out the door when Amit

arrives. Mum and Dad don't like visitors apart from family. They don't really trust them. And I feel the same if you really want to know.

Mum's packed sandwiches and cake for me. She puts it all on the table, goes upstairs, and comes down with her pink hat, the one with the net on it.

"Can I come, AJ?" she says. "I'm not working till this afternoon."

I'm a bit shocked to tell you the truth.

"Actually," I hear myself say, "could you not?"

"Yes I can," she says. "My boy is in a special race."

"Please don't come," I say.

"Why?"

I can't speak.

"I won't wear the hat," she says, and she puts it down.

"It's not the hat," I say.

"Is it because of parents evening?"

She's waiting for an answer and I can't think what to say. I could tell her it's going to be really boring or she won't like it but neither is true.

"Yes," I say.

Mum's face goes completely flat. Dad comes in and stands behind her. He's looking at the floor. There's a car honking outside. Then the doorbell goes.

"That'll be Amit," I say.

We stare at one another.

The bell goes again. I run to the door and Mum follows. Amit's standing on the step. Mum's behind me and I'm sort of trapped between them. Then Dad comes and stands behind Mum.

"Well," says Mum, "if you don't want me to come you can still take this." She shoves my packed lunch into my hands.

Amit looks past me and smiles at Mum and Dad. Then we run to the car.

When we get in the car Amit's mum says, "Do your parents want a lift? We do have room."

"No thanks," I say. "It's not their thing."

If I could disappear down between the seats, I would.

"Well, good for you," she says, "for doing it anyway."

She looks so strong and confident and she's wearing perfume or something and it's making me feel sick. Or maybe I feel sick because of what I just did. I couldn't let Mum come because she can be so embarrassing. And I'm embarrassing enough on my own.

COLLAPSIBLE CHAIR

There's loads of schools at the event, all set up across the field in little groups with gazebos. Mr. Higgins has a green flag on the top of his.

"Green for go," he says.

We wait around for hours. I feel sick the whole time and I can't blame Amit's mum's perfume because she's sitting across the field. She's brought a collapsible chair and a thermos and every now and then she pours herself a drink.

Amit jogs around and does some push-ups and when he's had enough he sits next to me.

"Why didn't you bring your mum?" he says.

I don't answer. I can't.

"She looked nice."

"She is nice," I say.

"She can have a lift with Mum another time if you want," he says.

I look at Amit's mum all confident and calm and I can't imagine her and my mum together. She puts her cup down on the grass and pulls a long woolly scarf out of her bag and it somehow gets tangled in her chair. She has to stand up to free it. It takes her ages. Amit winces.

"All parents are embarrassing," he says.

I don't want to talk about parents so I ask Amit what he's done with the Olympic tickets. He's got them in the frame on his wall.

"I look at them every day," he says.

When it's our race I run my fastest ever. I want to get it over with as soon as possible and I want to get through to the next round so Mum can come and wear her pink hat and wait at the finish line. And with every step I'm wishing I was someone else, someone better. Amit's close behind me and this other boy who runs like a terrier, but I don't let them pass.

I'm first over the line. The terrier boy is right behind me and then there's Amit. My heart feels like it's going to burst out of my chest. My legs are shaking. Amit pats me on the back.

Mr. Higgins jogs over. He's got his arm in the air before he gets to us, ready to high-five. And he comes to me first!

"Brilliant!" he says.

He slaps his hand against mine and then Amit's and then against his chest.

"Proud," he says.

We're through to the borough trials. I can hardly believe it. I'd be walking on air if I was a nicer person.

SOMETHING BAD

Mum's pink hat's still on the table when I get in. Mum and Dad are in the kitchen. They look scared.

"What's happened?" I say.

"Nothing, AJ," says Mum.

She slides something into Dad's gardening drawer.

"How was the race?" she says.

"Good," I say. "I'm through to the borough trials. I might get into the London Youth Games. Will you come if I do? And if I win you can throw your hat in the air, like people did in the olden days."

I pick up the hat and throw it into the air and catch it. Mum laughs but it's not a real laugh. She's standing under a cloud.

"Please," I say.

She puts her arms around me.

"Maybe," she says.

I wonder what she's hiding. It could be something for my birthday but it doesn't feel like that. It feels like something bad.

WEIRD AND AMAZING AND TERRIBLE

It's awards night and Mum's coming and I don't even care what happens. Well, I do care a bit, but I'm not going to let it show. We get to the hall early because prizewinners sit at the front and I want Mum close in case she gets worried. She sits right behind me. She can't stop smiling.

The ceremony's not the most exciting thing in the world. The worst bit is when an old man who was at school about a hundred years ago tells us what it used to be like (blackboards instead of whiteboards and fountain pens with bottles of ink instead of computers). Then one of the school governors talks about a new science lab and by the time she's finished my brain's left the hall completely and I'm imagining myself triumphing at the borough tryouts (I've won the race without breaking a sweat).

Finally the headmistress calls out the winners starting with Year 7s and we take turns to go onstage and get a certificate and shake hands with everyone.

Mum's really excited. It would be awkward except there's loads of adults here and they're all more excited than the kids.

When my name's called Mum doesn't make a sound. As I walk onto the stage I pretend I'm about to step up to a podium to collect a medal (gold probably). I want to do a little wave at the crowd but I stop myself.

Harvey takes the longest time to get his certificate. He's loving every moment. Crystal marches onto the stage like she's done it a hundred times before. Amit gets a certificate for Science and manages to look really cool, which is quite annoying actually as he's not cool at all. (Anyone who washes away Usain Bolt's autograph can never be cool.) Then we wait forever while the names from the other years are read out.

I'm nearly asleep when the headmistress says "Anika Sharma." I shudder awake and check my feet to make sure I'm not wearing the running shoes (even though I know I'm not). A girl walks past me and onto the stage, a rope of black hair bouncing off her shoulders. She takes her certificate, shakes hands with everyone, turns around, and walks back to her seat. It's the girl from the convenience store! Anika Sharma is the girl from the convenience store! It's sort of unbelievable. I think my heart might break out of my chest.

I can't think of anything else the rest of the evening. All I can think about is me running around the park in Anika Sharma's shoes and me doing the cross-country race in Anika Sharma's shoes and me maybe even going into the convenience store in her shoes. And not even knowing. It's weird and amazing and terrible.

When we pile out of the hall Amit's mum taps my shoulder.

"Congratulations, AJ," she says.

Mum's beaming.

"This is my mum," I say.

"You must be very proud."

"I am," says Mum. "I'm very proud. Aren't I, AJ?"

They both smile—two mums proud of their kids.

We pass Anika Sharma standing in the foyer surrounded by people. I think she glances at me, though I could be wrong. She's smiling.

When we get outside Mum says, "Can we go to the river, AJ?"

"Yes, Mum."

By the time we get there the sky's filled with clouds. The stadium's glittering.

"I hope you've got your star," I say, "because I don't think we're going to see any.

Mum nods.

"I have," she says.

"Did you ever win a prize, Mum?"

She shakes her head.

"Well, I give you the prize for best mum in the world."

"Aw, thank you, AJ."

She leans her head on my shoulder. I know it's embarrassing and uncool but it's just me and Mum by the river looking for stars and I'm wishing the moment could last forever.

FINAL REMINDER

Some things you can never understand. When I go to bed I have this feeling that everything's exactly as it should be, like how could it be any other way? Because now that I know who Anika Sharma is and now that I know I've been wearing her shoes, it all makes a weird kind of sense. I think I'm the happiest boy in the world.

I fall asleep quickly but suddenly I'm wide awake and I'm remembering Mum sliding something into Dad's gardening drawer. It's buzzing around my head. I need to know what it was. I creep downstairs. There's no one up. The cat's sitting on the garden wall next to the pumpkin.

I put on the kitchen light and open Dad's drawer. It's full of string and seeds and stuff and there's a pile of letters on top. I take out the top one. The envelope's open. It's a bill from the water board, only this time it's red! It's got FINAL REMINDER written right across it in red capital letters. At the bottom it says *Total due: £122.46* and that's in red too. I take out the next one. It's a bill for our TV license and it's red too. At the top it says *Urgent—you risk breaking the law.*

I can't look anymore. I think I might be sick. I walk up and down the kitchen like Dad walks up and down the garden but I don't feel any calmer. When I'm too tired to think anymore I put the bills back. I'm going to do what Mum and Dad do. I'm going to close the drawer and try to forget they even exist.

NEARLY PERFECT

"Don't look," Aisha says. "It's a surprise."

She's drawing me a birthday card.

She's laid out her felt-tip pens in order of color.

"Do you think it'll be okay to have a new baby?" she says.

I don't know what to say. Because my real answer would be *No, I don't think it'll be okay at all.* I think it'll be rubbish.

"Ye-eah," I say. (I sort of stretch it out to make it less of a lie.) "You'll be a big sister."

"But what if the baby's noisy?"

"It will be noisy. They always are. You were the noisiest baby in the world."

"Was I?"

She's trying to find a felt-tip with some red left in it. She's making circles on a scrap of paper but no color's coming out.

"Was I sweet?"

"No. You were ugly. You kept dribbling and crying and you always had a big fat smelly diaper."

(I don't know why I'm being so nasty.)

She puts down her pen and sticks out her bottom lip. I'm not sure if she's annoyed about the color or annoyed about me.

"Did you like anything about me?" she says.

"No."

She's trying to outstare me.

"I'm only telling you to warn you," I say, "so if the new baby's a bit annoying you'll know it won't last. Because now you're nearly perfect."

"Nearly perfect?"

"Yeah, well, no one can be a hundred percent perfect. But you nearly are. There'll never be anyone as perfect as you."

"Not even the baby?"

"No way!"

I'm shaking my head and I'm not lying now. I believe it.

"How perfect am I? Like what?"

"Like a blue sky with no clouds."

And suddenly all the clouds have gone from her face.

"So the new baby will be okay."

I nod.

"In the end, yeah. Just remember what I said."

She gets back to her drawing. She doesn't want to talk anymore. She wants to concentrate.

When Mum comes in Aisha shows her the card and they both start sniggering. It's quite annoying to tell you the truth.

TRYING TO FORGET

One thing I've noticed is if you try to forget something you really can't. In fact, the more you try not to think about it the more it gets stuck in your head. I'm lying in bed trying not to think about the red bills in Dad's drawer but I can't think of anything else. I give up trying to sleep and go downstairs.

Dad's in the garden digging a hole. He's got a candle in an eggcup balanced on the wall. It's two o'clock in the morning. I open the kitchen door and stick my head out.

"Dad," I say.

He looks up.

"You're not burying Mum, are you?"

He bursts out laughing.

"No! No, no, Mum's in bed. I wouldn't do that!"

He can't stop laughing. He has to put his shovel down. He's leaning on the wall. It's funny because it's the most ridiculous thing in the world. Because he absolutely loves Mum.

"I'm digging in some compost," he says.

He's trying to pull his face into shape.

He comes in and we sit at the table and drink tea. We don't speak. We just sit. And all the time I'm thinking about the bills in the drawer and whether I should say something. But in the end I don't.

COLD BAKED BEANS

We're making breakfast when the electricity goes off. There's still no money in the jar and the arrow on the meter points to Empty. I tell Mum we need more coins. Her face is frozen.

"I don't get paid till next week," she says at last.

My stomach's lurching like I'm on a really fast fairground ride and I'm being spun upside down. Mum and Dad look like they're on the same ride except no one's smiling and no one's screaming. We just want to get off.

Eventually Mum gets out a tin of baked beans. We eat them cold but it's nothing like the picnic we had in the garden. It's no fun at all because now we've got a problem. Mum's wringing her hands like they do in films to show how worried the character is. And Mum wringing her hands makes me wring my hands too. Only I'm doing mine inside my head.

I wring my hands in my head all day at school. I can't think about anything else except how we can manage without electricity for a week. I never thought much before about how it keeps everything going. Crystal and Harvey try to talk to me but I can't really hear what they say. My brain feels like scrambled egg. At the end of the day I race out the school gates. Amit waves to me from the track but I pretend not to see.

I'm really, really hoping the lights will be on when I get home, but of course they're not. I put the running shoes I got from school into a plastic bag (trying not to look at them because I like them so much) and I take them down to Easy Exchange.

DIAMOND EARRINGS

There's a saxophone in the window of Easy Exchange. It's dented and dusty but I bet if it could talk it would have loads of stories to tell. I've walked past the shop twice already so I've had lots of time to think about the saxophone. And now I'm thinking, *I can't walk past the shop another time. I have to go in or I have to go home.* I grit my teeth and walk in.

There's an old man behind the counter.

"I've got some running shoes," I say. "Size six."

I take them out of the bag. A man in a baseball hat turns around to see.

The old man picks them up.

"Not bad," he says.

"They're new," I say. "They've hardly been worn."

"And you're over eighteen, are you?"

I nod.

"What are you? A student?"

I nod.

"Nursery or primary school?" he says.

"Ha-ha," I say.

"Let's see your ID then."

"I've forgotten it."

He shrugs.

"Come back with your ID. Or when your voice has broken."

I feel terrible. I'm never coming in here ever again. Even if the most perfect thing is in the window and it would save my life or even save the world and I've got enough money in my pocket I will never, ever come in this shop again.

I put the shoes back in the bag and walk out, keeping my head down in case I see anyone I know. There have been lots of embarrassing moments in my life but this is the worst ever. One million percent.

The man in the baseball hat follows me out and steps in front of me.

"How much d'you want?" he says. "I'll give you a fiver."

"Um. They cost about eighty pounds in the shop."

"Well, take them back to the shop then."

I give him my death stare. He takes out a five-pound note.

"Take it or leave it. Not diamond earrings, are they?"

I can't believe there's a single diamond earring in the shop. Or even a single diamond, or a bit of gold that isn't fake or a pearl. It's all just old stuff that no one wants. Except somebody always wants it. Probably the person taking it in.

I give him the shoes and take the money. As I walk away I feel so bad. I'm not sure if I've just saved the day or ruined my future. I might even have committed a crime.

SLOT MACHINES

The bank's empty apart from a woman in a suit sitting behind a glass screen. She looks bored stiff.

"Can I have this in pound coins?" I say.

I give her the five-pound note.

"Of course," she says.

She's suddenly beaming. I think she's glad to have a customer. It must be crazy-boring sitting behind that screen all day.

"We usually have kids wanting to change coins into notes," she says. "You're doing it the other way around."

She puts the note in a drawer. There's a whole wedge of them.

"I always do things the other way around," I say.

She counts out five coins.

"What are you going to do with them? Slot machines?"

I shake my head.

"Good," she says. "Slot machines are a terrible waste of money. Do you have a bank account?"

"No, I'm eleven," I say.

"Never too early to start," she says. Her teeth

are gleaming. "You could open one if you like and we could put this in. Better than slot machines."

"It's not for slot machines."

"I see."

She's suddenly quite annoying.

"I'm going to buy a bucket," I say, "to put over my head."

(Don't ask me why I say that. It just pops out.)

She puts the five coins in a little plastic bag and pushes them under the glass.

"You do know you should never put anything over your head?" she says.

I drop my mouth open as far as I can and stare at her. She raises her eyebrows.

"Will that be all?" she says.

"Yes, thank you."

I take the plastic bag and go.

CANDLES

Dad's heating potato-and-onion soup over Grandad's camping stove.

"Cup of tea, AJ?" Mum says. "We can heat some water, can't we, Eddie?"

"No thanks," I say.

I don't give them the money straightaway, even though they could really do with it, because I don't want to lie to them. I have to work out what to say so it isn't exactly a lie because if I start lying to them everything will be terrible.

I go up to my room, sit on my bed, and look out at the darkening sky. A hundred things are racing through my head, like what if the school finds out I sold the shoes and calls social services or even the police and what if I don't get shoes for my birthday and what would Mr. Higgins do if he found out? It's a relief when Mum calls me down for tea.

There's a candle on the kitchen windowsill and three bowls of soup on the table. I sit down and start to eat and then I drop my spoon, pick it up, and get up for a clean one. As I take the spoon out of the cutlery drawer I push the coins right to the back, count to ten, and pull them out again.

"Look at this!" I say.

"What?" says Mum.

"Pound coins."

"Pound coins?"

"Yes," I say. "There's five, I think."

Mum looks like she's smiling.

"Grandad must have put them there," she says. "That's the sort of thing he'd do."

"Shall I put them in the meter?" I say.

"Yes!" says Mum. "Isn't that lucky, Eddie?" she says.

I put all five coins in the meter and everything springs back to life. The lights are on and the fridge is whirring. Dad looks worried. I feel sick.

FINGERS CROSSED

It's the trials next week and my birthday tomorrow and I'm keeping my fingers crossed every moment I can in the hope I'll get new running shoes. It's not easy, I can tell you. Even simple things like holding a knife and fork are nearly impossible when your fingers are crossed. Mum gets annoyed because I keep slopping tea onto the table. She says she's going to dig out my old baby cup.

I'm back to training on the stairs. I do eighty-three times now. That's eighty-three times up the stairs and eighty-three times down, in case you hadn't realized. It's my age and Grandad's age added together and it's absolutely the most I can do. When I finish I collapse onto the bottom step and talk to myself in

French like before. Only now I go shopping in the market (*au marché*) and buy fish (*des poissons*), cheese (*du fromage*), and apples (*des pommes*).

FAST

Mr. Higgins has got this amazing new sports car. It's an electric-blue convertible. He's sort of in love with it. He glances back when he walks away, like he just has to steal another look.

Harvey sees it as we're walking to PE. His eyes nearly fall out of his head. It's a bit embarrassing to be honest.

"Wow," he says. "I'm getting one of those when I'm grown-up. I'm getting a red one."

I don't say it but I can't help thinking if anyone's going to get one of those it'll be me with my amazing running ability.

When Harvey starts taking selfies next to it I have to walk away. He really is an embarrassment. I've been avoiding Mr. Higgins all week and I don't want him to see me drooling over his car.

Mr. Higgins is waiting outside the changing room.

"I think I've pulled a muscle," I say.

"Oh," he says.

He's sort of bouncing on the spot.

"Well, get some rest then. No problem."

"Do you want me to clean your office?" I say. "Sort some shoes or something?"

(I'm hoping someone's left another pair of sixes.)

"No thanks, AJ," he says. "You did a good job last time. All done."

I look at him imploringly, like it would make me feel so much better if I could do a job for him. It doesn't work.

"Don't worry," he says. "There's a few days till the trials. Give yourself a rest."

And that's it. I sit in the library because I can't bear to watch the other kids running around in PE, but then when I get there I stare out the window because I can't bear not to watch either.

As I walk out of school I see Amit running around the track. He's fast.

TWELVE YEARS OLD

I'm twelve years old today. We have pancakes for breakfast. I make my special lump-free batter. Mum puts her arms around me. She seems tiny.

"My boy," she says.

"Happy birthday, AJ," Dad says.

In tutor period Miss Charmant makes a fuss of me. She does it for everyone but it doesn't make it any less embarrassing.

"Let's sing 'Happy Birthday' for AJ," she says.

Harvey jabs his fingers into my back. It hurts. Everyone starts to sing and I feel myself getting hotter and hotter. I practically fly out of the classroom when the bell goes.

Crystal's brought in some ginger cake and we sit on the field at break and eat it. She's talking about not straightening her hair.

"What do you think?" she says.

I don't know what to think. The only thing in my head is: *Please can Josephine be wrapping a pair of running shoes for me?* And then I think, *What if Mum and Dad give me running shoes too?* It's going to be embarrassing if I get two pairs, especially if one is better than the other. And then I think, *Maybe I won't get any shoes at all.* When I think that I can hardly breathe. I cross my fingers and my cake falls onto the grass.

MORE BALLOONS

Mum and Dad are waiting in the kitchen when me and Aisha get back from school. They've blown up some balloons and Mum's made a chocolate cake. There's a present on the table. It's big enough to be running shoes but it doesn't look like a shoe box.

"For you," says Mum proudly.

It's a backpack with a camouflage pattern.

"Now you don't have to use Dad's," Mum says.

My heart's sinking. I have to take lots of deep breaths so I don't throw a wobbly and break the new teapot.

"Thanks very much," I say.

Aisha pulls a card and a present out of her bag. The card's got a drawing on it of me holding a baby. The baby looks exactly like me with long legs hanging out of a nappy. Everyone laughs.

"I've seen it before," says Mum proudly.

"Now open the present," says Aisha.

It's a bottle of shampoo with a picture of a horse on the front. It's called Glossy Mane. (Aisha usually gets me things she'd like herself.)

"It's got conditioner in it," says Aisha. "If you use it every day your hair won't look so dry."

"Thanks, Aisha," I say.

"Because it is a bit dry now," she says.

By the time Josephine and Tyler arrive I'm feeling desperate. They give me an MP3 player.

"We've got another present for you, haven't we, Tyler?" says Josephine. "Only not quite yet."

Tyler nods.

"It's to do with running," Aisha whispers.

I want to say *Could I have it soon?* or *Will I get it by Friday?* but that seems rude. So instead I say, "Well, you know where to find me."

It sounds a bit odd. Josephine laughs.

"That we do, AJ," she says.

Mum lights the candles on the cake and turns out the kitchen light and everyone starts to sing "Happy Birthday." I cross my fingers under the table because I've really, really got to get the running shoes soon. Like tomorrow.

And then the electricity goes off. The fridge stops whirring and the hall light goes out and we're standing in darkness apart from the circle of candles. Aisha screams and then because it sounds so good in the dark she keeps on screaming. Tyler puts on the flashlight on his phone.

"I'll check the trip switch," he says. "Where's your meter?"

"Under the stairs," I say.

He goes to check and comes back.

"You need to put some money in," he says. "What's it take?"

"Pound coins," I say.

Tyler's shaking out his pockets. Mum and Dad don't move.

"What's happening, Alice?" says Josephine.

Mum doesn't answer. No one does.

"Right," says Tyler, "I'll go to the shop and get some change."

Josephine taps me on the shoulder.

"AJ," she says, "a word?"

GAMBLING AND FANCY CLOTHES

Me and Josephine are standing under a lamppost. Josephine looks really overheated and really worried. I hope she's okay. I so much don't want her to have the baby out here on the pavement. Especially on my birthday.

"What's happening?" she says.

I know she won't go without an answer. She's like Mum in that way.

"Grandad used to bring the coins for the meter," I say, "but now we don't have any."

Now that I've started I can't stop.

"And we've got red bills. They're going to block our water pipes because we haven't paid the bill. And they might send us to prison for not paying the TV license."

Josephine puts her hands to her face. I can hear Aisha singing in the house. You need someone like Aisha when things go wrong. She's singing every version of "Happy Birthday"—*you look like a monkey, you look like an ostrich*. She's making them up as she goes along. I wish I was a monkey right now. I'd climb the highest tree and swing from one to the next, right through the jungle.

"Grandad didn't tell me how to look after the money," I say.

"You shouldn't be looking after the money! You're eleven." Josephine's nearly screaming.

"Twelve actually."

She calms down.

"Why didn't you tell me?"

"Mum said you've got too much to worry about."

And suddenly Josephine's crying.

"AJ," she says, "I'm sorry. It's been crazy since Grandad died. I didn't think."

"The thing is . . . ," I say.

Then the words pop out—one at a time with a full stop in front of each because that's the only way I can say them.

"I'm. Worried. I'll. Have. To. Go. Into. Foster. Care."

She answers with a full stop in front of each word too.

"No. No. Never."

"But Grandad's not here."

She puts her hands on my shoulders.

"I'm here," she says.

Tears are pouring down her cheeks. It reminds me of the funeral.

"Alice is still working, isn't she?"

I nod.

"Then nothing's changed. Unless they've taken up gambling or buying fancy clothes."

The thought of Dad gambling or wearing fancy clothes makes me smile. I shake my head.

"Then I just have to pick up where Grandad left off. Their money goes into a bank. I'll sort it out."

She touches my cheek.

"And you can keep being eleven."

"Twelve."

"Right," she says.

She takes out her purse and presses a twenty-pound note into my hand.

"Can you change this into coins?"

I nod.

"Okay," she says, "and from now on you give me the bills."

The candles are sinking into the cake in a sad, vanishing circle. We're all sort of watching. I can't look at Mum. Even in darkness I can tell there's a huge cloud over her. She's not meant to feel like this on my birthday. Josephine gives her a hug.

Tyler's in the hall slotting money into the meter. The hall light goes on and the fridge starts up again. He comes in and flicks on the kitchen light.

"Aw," says Aisha, "I liked the dark. It was fun."

She's got chocolate icing all over her face.

"Have you been at the cake?" says Josephine.

"No!" Aisha says.

The cake looks like it's been attacked by a squirrel.

"Can we sing 'Happy Birthday' again?" Aisha says. "Because last time was spoiled."

I think this is going to be really awful but there's something about Aisha with icing all over her face that makes it okay. And suddenly they're all singing. Josephine's stopped crying, Dad looks proud, Aisha's looking pleased with herself, Tyler—well, Tyler looks like Tyler—and Mum's singing loudest of all.

And me, I don't know whether to laugh or cry. I don't have to worry about bills anymore or the electricity or the water running out, but the trials are next week and I don't have any running shoes.

When they've all finished singing Tyler takes a photo of me.

"Come on, AJ," he says. "Any chance of a smile?"

I have to smile. He just put some money in our meter and he's promised me another present, probably running shoes. So I smile. And as I do Aisha bounces a balloon on my head.

"Can you believe it, Eddie?" says Mum. "Our boy, twelve years old."

SAVING FOR A FUTURE

I carry Josephine's twenty-pound note in my pocket all day, which is pretty stressful I can tell you. I have to keep checking it's there. After school I run to the bank. It's the same cashier as last time and she looks just as bored as before.

"Can I have this in pound coins?" I say.

She raises her eyebrows.

"It's not for slot machines, is it?"

"Nope."

"We had another boy come in asking for money for machines."

I nod.

"There you go."

She pushes the money under the glass.

"And take this too."

She pushes a leaflet through after the money. It's

got a picture on it of a boy in an armchair with his parents sitting either side and they're all smiling.

"Talk to your parents. It's never too soon to start saving for a future."

DEPOSIT PAID

I count the coins into the meter in French all the way up to twenty. (Yes, I can do that now.) We've got another bill so I put it in Dad's drawer for when Josephine comes over next. But as I try to shut the drawer something keeps it from closing. I push my hand to the back and pull out a scrunched-up bit of paper. It's a receipt from the Choc Box and it says, NOVELTY RUNNING SHOE, DEPOSIT PAID.

I look at it for ages because I can't make sense of it. It must be from when Grandad ordered my chocolate running shoe but I don't understand why it's in Dad's gardening drawer. I look out into the garden. Dad's shoveling compost into a bucket. He looks up and when he sees me he nods. And then I understand.

I open the door and go outside.

"Dad," I say, "I found this. It's a receipt for the chocolate running shoe."

He sort of shudders. He can't look at me.

"Did you get it for me?" I say.

He doesn't move for a few moments and then he speaks.

"Grandad took me to the chocolate shop to order it," he says, "but when he died I couldn't pick it up."

He looks so upset I want to scream, for all the things we don't see and all the things we don't say. But instead I count up to ten and then back down again (in French) and then I smile. And it's not even a wobbly smile.

"Thank you!" I say.

I might even be shouting.

I run inside and grab the chocolate from the shelf where I hid it from Aisha.

"Let's finish it," I say.

We sit between the drooping sunflowers and break off little pieces.

"It's for starting secondary school," says Dad.

"It's the best present ever," I say.

A crumb falls onto the ground.

"The ants will get that," Dad says. "Watch."

I don't know how long we sit there, but we end up watching the ants in the light from the kitchen because it's gotten dark. They swarm over the chocolate and carry it away.

THE DAY BEFORE THE TRIALS

It's Thursday and I still don't have any running shoes for the borough trials. Josephine's been working late so she hasn't come to pick up Aisha since my birthday. Tyler comes instead but he just runs in, grabs Aisha, and he's gone again. I asked Aisha when I'll get my present and she said, "They do have other things to worry about, you know." (Which was kind of embarrassing.)

I've stopped walking across the school field. I go around the edge because I don't want to see Mr. Higgins or Amit. I don't want them to ask how I am.

And one of the worst things is I can't walk out of school with Crystal because she won't really want to skirt the edge of the field like a spy. And I don't want to explain. I don't want to tell anyone. It just feels too bad.

Crystal's getting pretty fed up with me to be honest. She's got a sort of annoyed face when she looks at me. We're walking down the corridor and she's talking to me but I can't really concentrate.

"Well, what do you think, AJ?" she says.

She stops and stares at me. I don't know what she's talking about. She shakes her head angrily and her hair springs around her face. She hasn't straightened it for ages and I haven't even noticed. To tell you the truth I don't think I'd have noticed if the roof had blown off the school and we were walking under sky.

"You know, AJ," she says, "not everything's about you."

And she stomps away. I feel so bad. I want to run after her and tell her it looks great (which it honestly does) but I feel so bad I'm sort of frozen. I can't wait for this week to be over. I can't imagine how it's going to end but if I'm not careful I won't even have my best friend. I keep my fingers crossed all day, hoping I'll get the shoes in time. It's not easy when you're holding a pen.

STRINGY MOP

Dad's waiting at the window when I come in from school.

"Mum's gone," he says.

He looks worried.

"She made a cake, put it in the tin, and now she's gone. She didn't say where she was going."

"When did she go?"

"About ten minutes ago," he says. "AJ, her hands were shaking."

"I'll find her," I say.

I put down my bag and walk casually out the front door and then I'm running. She must have gone to the café in the park. I can't think of anywhere else. I hope it's not shut. I hope they don't laugh at her. I hope she doesn't change her mind when she gets there. It's getting dark. I imagine her sitting on a bench not sure what to do.

Victor walks out of the gate as I run in.

"Have you seen my mum?" I say.

"Café," he says.

I run to the café and peer through the window. It's shut but the lights are on. Mum's sitting at a table with a group of people. The woman with hoop earrings comes to the door.

"AJ," she says, "come in. We're just tasting your mum's delicious cake."

Mum looks up. She's absolutely beaming. I stand around awkwardly while they finish.

"Would you like to do some mopping, AJ?" says the woman.

"Uh, no thanks."

"He used to love mopping, didn't you, sweet-heart?" she says. "He loved that big stringy mop."

Everyone laughs. Mum too. She actually laughs louder and longer than anyone.

They buy the cake. The whole thing. They're going to sell the rest in the café. And they want her to make one for the weekend. It's like Mum's suddenly grown two feet taller. All the way home she can't stop smiling.

"I did it by myself," she says.

"What made you go?"

"It was seeing Aisha singing 'Happy Birthday' with cake all over her face. It made me think people love my cakes."

She looks up at me.

"And you being twelve years old, AJ," she says. "You won't need me to look after you soon. So I'd better look after myself."

Dad's waiting at the door when we get home.

"I sold my cake," Mum says.

And a whole ray of sunshine is pouring down on her head.

WHAT WOULD YOU BE?

"If you were a bit of nature, what would you be?" Aisha says.

"Don't know."

"Think."

I'm frowning to make it seem as though I'm thinking hard but actually my mind's completely blank.

Aisha walks over and takes my hands.

"Think harder," she says.

"What do you mean? Like a tree?"

"Yes. Maybe a tree but don't just say that because it's the first thing you think of."

"Okay."

I'm thinking. She's stepping from foot to foot. She's impatient.

"What about you?"

"You first," she says. "Go on, tell me."

It's not as if I'm keeping something to myself. I just don't know. I'm running all sorts of things through my head—trees, hedges, mountains. None of them seem quite right.

"Sea," I say at last.

"Sea?"

"Yeah. Sea."

"Why?"

"Because I'm a deep thinker."

"Deep like the sea?"

"Yes."

She looks annoyed.

"The sea's too big to be just one person."

"Is it?"

"Yes. It nearly covers the whole world."

"Tell me what you'd be, Aisha."

"I'd be...you know one of those bits that float

down and spin around and around. They look like fairies when they're flying."

"And if you plant them you get a tree?"

Her face is angry.

"Yes, but I don't mean the tree. I mean the bit with the seed that spins around."

"Go on then," I say. "Show me."

So suddenly she's a seed swirling through the air. And I'm thinking, *I'm a volcano*. I know it looks like a hill on top with fluffy clouds drifting all around but actually I'm full of bubbling boiling rage and I'm glad Aisha's spinning. It calms me down. Because it's the borough trials tomorrow and I don't have running shoes and I don't want Aisha to go home because she takes my mind off things. And I know Tyler won't bring the shoes tonight. I just know it.

And he doesn't. He doesn't even come in. He stays in his car and honks his horn and Aisha goes running out.

TURN BACK TIME

I'm lying on my bed with my head under the pillow. I'd like to stay here forever, well, not forever, just until I'm fourteen, say, when everything might be sorted out.

I'm trying to think of a plan to get out of the trials tomorrow. I could set off the fire alarm so the school has to be evacuated, but Mr. Higgins might still put me on the minibus. I could miss school but he might come to our house. I could say I've still got an injury but I don't think he'd believe me. I'm going to have to act like I'm not interested, like I really don't care. Except I care so much I think my heart is going to burst out of my chest and start bashing itself on the walls.

Mum comes up and sits on the bed and pats my shoulder like you do with a little kid. And in that moment I would do anything to turn back time. I think of all the things I'd give up if I could have Grandad back—collecting conkers, riding on his shoulders from school, seeing Usain Bolt win the 100 meters. But then I think if I gave up all the things we did together, it would almost feel like he hadn't been here at all. And then I don't know what to think.

"What's wrong, AJ?" Mum says.

I don't answer.

"Would you tell Grandad what's wrong?"

I don't know what to say so I shake my head. Mum gets up and draws the curtains. Then she kisses my hair, the bit that's sticking out from under the pillow.

"Remember to be kind," she says, "to yourself as well."

And she's gone. It sounds like really good advice but I don't know what to do with it.

FOXES

It's five in the morning and I'm standing at my window. It's amazing what goes on in the street at night.

Three foxes run in and out of people's gardens, sniffing the trash bins and pulling out plastic bags. Every now and then they have a little standoff. If they find something to eat, they drag it behind a bicycle shed.

A man and woman come out of a house and sit on their wall and smoke cigarettes. They don't speak. They just sit next to each other and look into the distance. An old man comes out and starts washing his car windows. I'm not kidding! It's dark and he's trying to shine his windows. A man with a briefcase glides down the road on a scooter, then comes back the other way a few minutes later. He nods at the couple on the wall. And all the time the foxes are running up and down the pavement and darting across the road.

Just as it gets light the milk truck arrives. It makes a funny high-pitched noise. The milkman leaves milk on some doorsteps and when he's gone the foxes snuffle around the bottles. Finally I hear Dad go downstairs and put the kettle on. It's time to get dressed.

BOROUGH TRIALS

I don't bother to eat breakfast. I'm too nervous and anyway, what's the point? I don't need to think about running on empty. I won't be running at all. I take my PE kit and old running shoes to school (don't ask me why) and I set off late so I won't see Crystal. When

I get to class I sit with my head down and don't say anything, except to nod when Miss Charmant takes attendance. Crystal and Harvey keep looking at me.

Mr. Higgins pops his head around the door.

"Excuse me," he says, "I just wanted to tell AJ to be at the sports hall at ten o'clock. The minibus leaves at ten thirty."

He's beaming at Miss Charmant.

"Big day," he says, and he's gone.

He sounds like he's jogging down the hall.

"Well done, AJ," Miss Charmant says, "and good luck."

Everyone's looking at me. I'm trying not to shrug.

I don't say a word until class is over and then I run into the corridor. Crystal grabs me. She's followed by Harvey.

"What's the matter?" she says.

She doesn't look angry anymore.

"I sold my shoes," I say. "I can't run."

Crystal's mouth falls open.

"Oh, AJ!" she says.

"It doesn't matter," I say.

I'm trying to smile. It's not easy. She knows it matters.

As the students pour into the corridor I see Mr. Higgins walking toward me. He's trying to get through a group of kids.

"I need to hide," I say.

"The toilets," says Harvey. "I'll keep him talking."

I race down the corridor and dart into the toilets.

As the door closes I hear Harvey say, "Excuse me, sir, did you hear about the boy who swallowed a magnet?"

Mr. Higgins's voice is booming.

"For goodness' sake, boy, get to your lesson."

I lock myself in a cubicle, put the lid down, and sit on it. I think of Tyler hiding in the toilets all night at the Oval just to watch the cricket match and I think how cool he was and I know I will never, ever tell him about this. Not ever.

UN-AC-CEPT-A-BLE

If you've ever had to hide in a toilet you'll know that after a while the smell sort of leaks into your blood. When I can't stand it anymore I come out of the cubicle and stand around reading the slogans. One says YOU CAN DO MORE THAN YOU THINK YOU CAN. GO OUT AND DO IT! Someone's written *poo* across both of the *do*'s. Any other day it would be funny.

I peer into the corridor. There's no one around so I set off for my Science class. I'm going to ask to go to the medical room. I'm about to open the door to the lab when a voice shouts my name.

"AJ!"

I turn around. It's Mr. Higgins.

"Where have you been? We're waiting."

He's towering over me. Not in a vertical way—we're about the same height—but in a horizontal way. He's about three times as wide as I am. I never noticed before. He's never been this close.

"I was in the toilets," I say. "I'm ill."

"You don't just not turn up," he says. "What are you thinking?"

He stares at me for ages, like if he looks hard enough he might see my thoughts.

"Where's your kit?"

"In my bag."

"Show me."

I take out my shorts and top. He takes the bag from me and pulls out my old running shoes with the rubber hanging off.

"Where are the new ones?" he says. "The ones you got here?"

"They don't fit."

"They fit better than these."

"They fell apart."

"They were new."

I shrug.

"This is all you've got with you?"

I nod.

"So you can't run today!"

I shake my head. He looks like he might explode. All that testosterone is swirling around.

"This will not do," he says. "It is UN-AC-CEPT-A-BLE. I will be speaking to your parents."

He marches back down the corridor. I'm trying not to imagine what his face must look like.

I run back to the toilet, fill a sink with cold water, and dip my face in it. Then I look at myself in the mirror. I look terrible. A sign above the mirror says A BAD ATTITUDE IS LIKE A FLAT TIRE; YOU'LL NEVER GO ANYWHERE UNTIL YOU FIX IT. The words are sitting right above my face. They remind me of a photo I saw once of a Victorian boy. He had a little sign in his lap saying PICKPOCKET AND THIEF.

I lock myself in a cubicle and try not to breathe too deeply. I'm going to sit here until I'm absolutely sure the minibus has gone. I'm trying not to cry.

"WHAT-IFS"

I miss three lessons and you know what, I don't care. Crystal and Harvey try to make me laugh but they can't. I'm not even sure what they're saying. I can't concentrate. I don't think I'll ever laugh again.

My head is full of *what-ifs*. What if Mr. Higgins tries to ring Grandad? What if Miss Charmant finds out I lied on the form? What if the school calls the police? What if social services think Mum and Dad can't look after me properly and take me away? What if Anika Sharma finds out I sold her shoes?

As soon as the bell goes I race out of school. It's starting to rain. Amit's standing next to the minibus with a group of kids in PE uniforms. They're back from trials. I pretend not to see him.

I'm a few streets from home when Mr. Higgins

passes me in his blue convertible. I've never seen him around here before. I bet he's going to my house. In fact, I'm sure he is. I have to stop Dad from answering the door.

I pretend I'm running for my life, which isn't that difficult because maybe I am. My shoes are slipping, rain's pouring down my nose, and even though it's cold I'm sort of on fire. And as I run a voice comes into my head—*There's a blizzard coming over the mountains, Grandad. I'm going to get the horses in.* And it goes around and around in my head and I don't even know why.

LEMON SHERBETS

Mr. Higgins's car is parked outside our house. He's standing on our doorstep. Dad's holding the door open not very wide and Mr. Higgins hasn't got his foot in the door exactly but he's got an imaginary foot in the door. Dad looks worried.

"AJ," he says when he sees me.

"Any chance I could come in for a moment?" Mr. Higgins says.

And without waiting for an answer he walks inside.

"This is Mr. Higgins," I say to Dad. "My PE teacher."

Dad looks like he's shrinking. He pulls off his hat. It's so strange to see him standing next to

Mr. Higgins with his hair sticking out all over the place. I wonder who's stronger. I imagine them doing an arm wrestle and wonder who'll win. A bit of me wants to say, let's sort things out with an arm wrestle.

"This is my dad," I say.

Mr. Higgins holds out his hand and shakes Dad's. Dad looks surprised. I'm sure a teacher's never shaken his hand before. We all stare at one another.

"Do you want to talk to AJ?" Dad says.

"Well, I actually wanted to talk to you or his grandfather."

"Grandad's dead," says Dad.

"Oh," says Mr. Higgins.

The whole world's falling in and all Mr. Higgins says is "oh."

"We're very sad about it," Dad says.

Mr. Higgins looks at me, then back at Dad.

"When did he die?"

"In the summer," Dad says.

"Well, perhaps I could talk to you," says Mr. Higgins.

Dad nods.

"Would you like some soup?" he says.

Mr. Higgins looks surprised.

"No, no thanks," he says. "I'm fine. I'm just here because AJ didn't come to the borough trials today."

"Running trials," I say.

"AJ had a place to compete. But he didn't show up. In fact, he hid in the toilet. It's quite special to get a place in the trials. If I'd known he wasn't coming someone else could have taken his place."

Dad frowns.

"Why didn't you go, AJ?" he says.

"My shoes don't fit."

"I gave you shoes," says Mr. Higgins.

Dad looks surprised.

"AJ very kindly cleared out the lost property for me so I said he could take a pair of shoes for himself. Where are they, AJ?"

"I can't wear them anymore."

I'm treading a fine line. I'm trying to be surly to Mr. Higgins while being friendly to Dad.

"Anyway," I say, "they're girls' shoes."

"They're still running shoes, AJ—as you know," says Mr. Higgins. "Have you any more excuses?"

I shake my head. They're both staring at me.

"Can I have them back then? So someone else can use them."

Mr. Higgins sort of smiles. He knows he's trapped me.

"I don't have them anymore," I say.

"Where are they?" says Dad.

I can't look Dad in the eye and lie to him so I tell the truth.

"I sold them," I say.

"What?"

Mr. Higgins looks furious. Everything's about to come crashing down.

"Why, AJ?" says Dad.

I don't know what to say so I say nothing.

"Is that where you got the money for the meter?" Dad says.

I nod. I'm so ashamed. Mr. Higgins shudders like he's just realized what an idiot I am. Nothing will ever be good again.

"The fridge wasn't working," I say. "And we couldn't cook and...I thought I'd get shoes for my birthday."

"We've got money for your shoes, AJ," says Dad. "We've got it in a tin upstairs."

"Couldn't you have put that in the meter?" says Mr. Higgins.

"No," says Dad. "It's for AJ. We save bills, not coins, so we can't put them in the meter."

Mr. Higgins is stepping from foot to foot.

"Wait," says Dad.

He runs upstairs and I can hear him shuffling around up there.

"My aunt Josephine's sorting things out now," I say. "She's having a baby. She stops work this week. She's going to do all the money things for us."

Mr. Higgins nods. He doesn't look impressed. He looks confused.

"She's a bookkeeper," I say. "That doesn't mean she looks after books. It means she looks after money."

Mr. Higgins nods again.

"I know," he says.

Dad comes running down with a candy tin like

the one under my bed only this one's got pictures of lemon sherbets on it. He puts it on the table.

"This is for you, AJ," he says. "It's for you."

He takes off the lid. It's full of notes. If Crystal was here, she could probably say how much there is just by looking. I'd have to take it out and count it but I can tell there's lots. There might even be a hundred pounds. Dad looks worried.

"Is it enough?" he says.

Mr. Higgins nods.

"That will be more than enough."

No one speaks. The silence feels like a bit of elastic being stretched and stretched.

"Well," says Mr. Higgins, "it looks like you're sorted."

"How much did you sell the shoes for, AJ?" Dad says.

"Five pounds," I say.

Mr. Higgins winces.

"We can give you the money," Dad says to Mr. Higgins. "I don't want AJ to get into trouble."

Mr. Higgins shakes his head.

"No need," he says. "He's not in trouble. Forget it. Really."

"Will you tell social services?" I say.

"No. Why would I do that?"

"Because Grandad's not here anymore and he used to help. Because if you do, I'm telling you now, I'm staying here anyway. With Mum and Dad."

"What?"

"I'm staying here."

And now my voice is cracking because of all the things that matter in the world to me, that matters most.

"I won't be telling social services, AJ," Mr. Higgins says. "If you can sort this out with your aunt, that sounds good to me."

He sighs.

"And maybe you need to talk to your dad a little more."

He reaches out to shake Dad's hand again. All the anger's gone out of him. He looks exhausted.

"I'm sorry to have bothered you," he says.

I follow him into the hall.

"Well, AJ," he says, "I'll see you Monday."

"I'm too late for the trials, aren't I?"

He nods.

"Yes. But there's always Year 8. And there's the summer athletics. What's your best distance?"

"I don't know."

"Well, we'll find out. But if you have any complicated domestic issues involving shoes, talk to me."

I nod.

"Right," he says.

He takes a deep breath. I think he's going to say STRIVE—*strength, tenacity, rigor, impetus, values, energy.* It'll be depressing if he does because the conversation's actually gone very well.

But instead he says, "Sorted then."

And he's gone.

ARM WRESTLE

I'm hoping if I stand in the hall long enough, Dad will go into the garden. But he's waiting for me.

"Is it all right now?" he says.

I nod.

"I'm sorry, Dad," I say.

"Me too," he says.

There's nothing for him to be sorry for but I don't say it because he wouldn't believe it.

"If we don't have to worry, maybe we don't need to tell Alice," says Dad.

"We don't have to worry," I say.

"And you can get new running shoes."

"Yes."

"You know," he says, "I was proud of the way you talked to that teacher. I was thinking—my boy talking to his teacher like that."

"Who do you think would win in an arm wrestle?" I say. "You or Mr. Higgins?"

He laughs.

"Your teacher," he says. "He's much stronger than me."

"I bet he isn't."

When Mum gets in Dad's just beaten me for the eighth time in an arm wrestle, four times each arm.

"Ooh," she says when she sees the lemon sherbet tin. "You've got AJ's money out."

"He needs shoes," Dad says.

"Okay," she says. "What color do you want, AJ?"

"He needs to buy them himself, Alice."

"No he doesn't. That's my job."

"No, Alice. It's his job now. They have to fit perfectly. He's got a big race on."

"Have you?"

"Well," I say. "Next year."

Her eyes are wide.

"Next year! AJ! That must be a big race! Make sure they're perfect," says Mum.

"You can go tomorrow," Dad says.

I'd like to cry. I'm not quite sure why, but anyway I'm not going to. I'm going to get new running shoes tomorrow and when I've got them I'm going to run and run and run and every time my foot hits the ground I'll be a little bit stronger. Until eventually I'll be flying.

RICHEST KID IN THE WORLD

Crystal comes shopping with me. I think it's going to take ages but the first pair of running shoes I try are exactly right. It's like they've been sitting in their box in the shop storeroom just waiting for me to put them on. Because they're absolutely perfect. Nothing hurts, they've got no one's name in them, and there's no rubber hanging off the edges. And when I jog up and down the shop I sort of bounce.

"Wear them home," says Crystal.

"What?"

"Put your other shoes in the box and wear these."

It's a bit embarrassing but I do. I have to stop

myself from swaggering out of the shop. They feel amazing.

We go to a café for hot chocolate and chips. And I pay! I feel like the richest kid in the world.

"I'm sorry I've been horrible," I say. "Your hair looks great."

"Don't worry," says Crystal.

She gets out a piece of paper and hands it to me. It's a drawing of a mandala.

"It was for your birthday but I didn't finish it in time," she says.

She's colored it all in. There are circles of footprints going around and around through grass and beside them is a spiraling river with fish jumping out. In the middle is a star and in the middle of the star it says *AJ*. It's really, really nice.

"Thank you," I say.

"You're welcome."

She's smiling.

"Do you think I'll be calmer now like you?" I say.

Crystal shakes her head.

"No."

BRILLIANT

I can tell everyone in PE's been talking about me. They're expecting me to be writing lines again or in detention or something and they're sort of surprised when Mr. Higgins doesn't treat me any different from the others.

When he sees my running shoes he nods. No one else would notice. It's for me. I think I know what it means. I think it means everything's okay.

When Amit sees me he runs over.

"What happened?"

"My shoes didn't fit."

He looks at my feet.

"New ones?"

I nod.

"How were the trials?" I say.

"I qualified," he says. "I was lucky you weren't there. Are you training after school?"

"Yes," I say.

I can't stop smiling.

When we train we jog for a bit and then we race. I don't even really try. I just love the feel of my feet on the track. But when we get to the finish I'm ahead. It's absolutely brilliant!

GRANDAD

I've run around the little park three times when Victor calls me over.

"I've got something for you," he says. "Just let me finish this."

He's eating a chicken-and-egg sandwich. It looks

revolting. Egg's falling out of his mouth and he's chewing really slowly.

"Tell me something," he says between mouthfuls. "What came first, the chicken or the egg?"

I shrug.

He sucks in the last bit of sandwich and pulls a black-and-white photo out of his pocket. It's Grandad next to the Canada Cup banner. He's holding a trophy.

"That's your grandad, that is," he says.

"I know," I say. "Why's he holding a trophy?"

"Because he won the race," says Victor.

"He didn't win."

Victor rolls his eyes.

"I think I'd know. I took the photo."

"But he didn't go to Canada."

"No. He met your nan. And as soon as he set eyes on her he didn't want to go."

I'm so surprised it takes me a while to understand. But then I think of the line of runners standing next to the banner and I look at Victor's photo of Grandad holding the trophy, and it all makes perfect sense. He looks like he's run the best race of his life.

"Did he ever wish he'd gone?" I say.

"Never!" says Victor.

"But his life was so hard."

"AJ," Victor says, "give me one word that sums up your grandad. One word."

My head fills with hundreds of words—*kind,*

funny, *organized*, *scruffy*, *tall*, *silly*...I put them into alphabetical order beginning with *amazing*, *brilliant*, *charming*. Victor's looking cold. He's eaten his sandwich and fed the ducks. He probably wants to go home. When I get to *H* I know the answer.

"Happy," I say.

He nods.

"Yes. He was happy," he says, and he smiles.

"What was it like when he won?"

"It was tight. He just pipped the other guy to the post. It was a fantastic race."

He gets up off the bench.

"So," he says, "do you want it or not?"

I'm nodding furiously.

We walk out of the park together, me holding the photo.

CANADA

Mum's so surprised when she sees Grandad holding the cup.

"He could have gone to Canada," I say.

"Why didn't he?" she says.

"Because he met Nan and he didn't want to leave her."

A huge smile spreads across her face.

"Oh, AJ," she says.

It's Friday evening and I'm already thinking about tomorrow's asteroid when the phone rings. I run downstairs. Mum and Dad are staring at it. I pick it up. It's Aisha. She sounds breathless.

"Mum's had the baby," she says.

"Did she?"

"Yes. And guess what—I delivered it."

"You? You're a superhero."

"Well, I didn't do all the work. Mum did some. It wasn't difficult. I've seen it on TV. I just kept Mum calm and told her to push. And after a while it came out."

"Wow!" I say.

"And I called 999."

"That's amazing."

"It was a bit bloody actually."

"I know. I've seen it on TV too," I say. "I'm glad I wasn't there."

I can hear a wobbly screech in the background.

"Is that it?" I say. "It sounds like a dying cat."

Aisha laughs.

"It's not like a cat at all," she says.

"Okay," I say. "Do you want to talk to Mum?"

"Yes, but wait," says Aisha. "Dad's switched his phone off. Mum thinks he's fishing. Can you get him?"

"Okay," I say.

I pass Mum the phone. She listens for a few moments and then she screams.

"Oh, Aisha! That's wonderful!"

And she hangs up.

FIFTY-FIFTY

Mum doesn't want me to go to the river on my own. She can't come because she's making a cake for the café. It's just gone in the oven.

"I'll be fine," I say.

"No you won't," she says. "It's dark."

Dad's looking pleased and worried at the same time.

"I'll come, AJ," he says.

He buttons up the collar of his coat and pulls his hat down. I grab my coat and we hurry out the door.

It's cold and dark and I can tell Dad feels more and more uncomfortable the farther we get from home. I keep close to him. When we get to the Olympic Park he gasps. The lights look so beautiful he can't help himself. We walk along the river. There's no one here but us.

"I've never been here in the dark," Dad says.

"Do you like it?"

He smiles uneasily.

"I think so."

Tyler jumps up when he sees us.

"Josephine's had the baby," I say. "Aisha was the midwife. They're at home."

He's having trouble understanding.

"Our Aisha delivered the baby?"

I nod.

"Are they okay?"

"They're fine."

He's looking from Dad to me and then back at Dad again. His mouth is open. He reels in his line, grabs his gear, and throws it all into his bag.

"Come on. I'll drop you home."

We follow Tyler back along the river. We're sort of running when he stops and spins around.

"What is it?" he says.

I don't know what he's talking about.

"Girl or boy?"

I don't know. I didn't ask. Dad's waiting for an answer too. He thinks I know but I don't. I'm thinking fifty-fifty. He's already got a girl so maybe he'll get a boy this time. I know it's a rubbish calculation.

"It's a boy!" I say.

What? Did I really just do that? Tyler makes a thumbs-up and runs on. I can't believe I get myself into these situations.

When we get to the car Dad gets in the front beside Tyler and I sit in the back on the smelly seat next to the fishing tackle.

"Thanks for coming out, Eddie," Tyler says. "I appreciate it. And you, AJ."

I grunt. I'm still worrying about the girl/boy thing. I get myself out of one kind of trouble and I fall straight into another.

When we get to our house Tyler says, "What are you doing in the morning, AJ?"

"Chores," I say.

"Do you want to come to the stadium?"

"What?"

Having another baby's been really good for him and he hasn't even met it yet. I can hardly breathe.

"Birthday treat," says Tyler. "It just took a while to fix."

"What about your job?" I say.

"It's okay. It'll be early though. I'll collect you at six. Can you get up that early?"

He doesn't need to worry about me sleeping in. I might not even go to bed.

"And wear your running shoes," he says. "You might get to stand on the track."

SCREAMY SORT

When we get in I call Josephine's cell phone. Aisha answers.

"Aisha," I say, "we found your dad. He's on his way home."

"Oh good, because we're getting fed up."

"What sort of baby is it?" I say.

"A screamy sort," she says.

"Is it a boy or a girl?"

"Um," she says.

She can sense power. She seems to wait forever.

"Aisha!" I shout.

"It's a boy," she says.

BABIES DON'T EAT CAKE

Mum's making another cake.

"This one's for the new baby," she says.

"New babies don't eat cake," I say.

She raises her eyebrows.

"I'm sure Aisha will."

Then she sighs.

"You know, AJ, you were the sweetest baby in the world."

"Was I?"

Dad nods.

"You were the prettiest you've ever been," says Mum.

They're both nodding now.

"Prettier than now?" I say.

"Twelve-year-old boys aren't very pretty, are they, AJ?" says Mum. She pats my arm. (She doesn't mean any harm.) "And you are twelve, aren't you?"

Dad sits down at the table. He's smiling.

"A new member of the family," he says.

AMAZING

I think I'm going to be awake all night but I fall asleep as soon as I hit the pillow. When I hear the milk truck I jump out of bed and start to race around doing my chores. And then I think, *You know what, I don't think the asteroid will hit our house today. I think it's going to be fine.* So I stop and have breakfast.

When Tyler arrives I run outside and jump in the front seat. Dad waves from the window. It's like I'm in a parallel universe: I'm wearing new running shoes, I've got a boy cousin, and Tyler's taking me to the Olympic Stadium. He's not exactly humming but his mouth is going up instead of down. He's not whistling, though he might be in his head.

"You must be happy to have a boy," I say.

"Well, if he's half the kid Aisha is I'll be happy."

We drive in silence. It's just getting light. I'm trying not to look too excited because Tyler's not that kind of person. And I don't want to be flattened because my heart is bursting.

When we get into the stadium Tyler takes me through a back door and gives me a security pass. It's got my photo on it, the one he took on my birthday just at the moment Aisha bounced a balloon on my head. The balloon's sitting on my head.

When we walk through the tunnel and come out in the stadium I can hardly believe my eyes. It's even bigger than I remembered. It's really unbelievable. I think I might faint. I'm not kidding. I reach around for something to hold on to but there's nothing there. Just a huge, amazing, incredible space. It's absolutely brilliant.

"Go on then," says Tyler.

"What?"

"Run."

He's gesturing at the track, looking a little impatient.

"Run!"

It takes me a while to catch my breath but then suddenly I'm running. I'm running around the track and it's red under my feet and it stretches out like a ribbon before me. And up above is the huge sky. I look out at the empty seats and as I turn the bend I look up at where we sat when we saw Usain Bolt and I do something I don't mean to. I lift my arm and I wave. And four small figures wave back. There's Mum, Dad, Grandad, and me and they all lift their hands and wave.

And then I'm flying. The ground is racing beneath my feet because I have to outrun the tears. They're pouring down my face but I can't stop because Tyler's at the end of the track and I don't want him to see me looking like this. So I have to do a whole other lap. My chest hurts and my heart's pounding in my ears. When I reach the bend again I look up and they've gone.

And when I finish my second lap I feel on top of the world, like everything makes sense and nothing can touch me. I can't stop smiling. It's like my mouth's peeled back and hung around my ears. It's a crazy smile.

Tyler's smiling too. Not quite like mine. Older I suppose. More worried about his job.

"Now scarper," he says.

He leads me back through the tunnel and out through the security area and takes my badge.

"Thank you," I say.

"Go on then," he says.

He presses a couple of pounds into my hand.

"And get yourself some breakfast."

I step outside and glance back and he's looking back too and very slightly smiling. Then he closes the door behind him.

MILLIONS OF PEOPLE

It's cold when I come out. I walk through the Olympic Park and stand on the bridge over the river. The sun's low and little bits of light are sitting on top of the water. I look at the flats and think of all the millions of people crammed into millions of buildings and how every one of them is a single life like Grandad's.

I stop at the convenience store on the way home. I want to get Mum some floury rolls. I hesitate before I go in because I'm really quite sweaty but Mum loves the rolls so I do.

Anika Sharma's standing behind the counter with the woman in the sari who might be her nan. They're sorting through a pile of newspapers.

"Have you got any floury rolls?" I say.

"One moment," the woman says. "How many?"

"Three."

She goes to the back of the shop and comes out with a tray of rolls, puts three in a paper bag, and hands them to me. I hold out my change but she shakes her head.

"First of the day," she says. "On the house."

I'm a bit embarrassed. I'm not sure why. I drop my change into my pocket and mutter thank you but I can't look up. I walk out of the shop all ugly and uncoordinated and then I glance back and they're both smiling at me. I wave.

And suddenly I'm really happy. I begin to run. As I'm running the change falls out of my pocket and I wonder for a moment who'll find it and whether they'll need it but then I'm not thinking about the change, I'm not thinking about anything. I'm just running. I'm running down the road at 50 miles per hour, 100 miles per hour even. I'm running so fast I'm almost flying and I picture myself up in the blue sky looking down on the stadium and the rivers and the cranes and our little park and Victor's bench and the house with the scruffy red door.

And behind the scruffy red door, home.

ACKNOWLEDGMENTS

Thank you to my family and friends as always for your patience, encouragement, and conversations, for reminding me I have a book to write and for finding me quiet corners to write in.

Thank you also to my agent Gillie Russell for your unwavering support and to all at Nosy Crow for continuing to believe in me. Big thank you in particular to Kirsty Stansfield for giving me confidence and helping me see the wood for the trees and to Rob Biddulph for the beautiful cover.

I spoke to many people while writing this book and am very grateful for all thoughts and advice. Most especially, I would like to thank the Huntesmith family and Our Group Your Group.